No Mate
or the
Magpie

Frances Molloy

Out of Ireland have we come.
Great hatred, little room,
Maimed us at the start.
I carry from my mother's womb
A fanatic heart.

W. B. Yeats
(Remorse for Intemperate
Speech)

First published by VIRAGO PRESS Limited 1985
41 William IV Street, London WX2N 4DB

Permission to reproduce the last verse of W. B. Yeats' 'Remorse for
Intemperate Speech' has been granted by Michael Yeats and Macmillan
London Ltd.

British Library Cataloguing in Publication Data

Molloy, Frances
  No mate for the magpie
  I. Title
  823'.914[F]   PR6063.0483/

  ISBN 0-86068-594-2
  ISBN 0-86068-599-3 Pbk

Typeset by Clerkenwell Graphics and
printed by Anchor Brendon, Tiptree, Essex

Frances Molloy was born in Derry, Northern Ireland in 1947. After what she calls 'a patchy education', she left school at fifteen to work in a local pyjama factory. In 1965 she spent a short time as a nun. Then in 1970 she decided to 'emigrate' to England. She now lives in Lancaster with her husband and two children.

Always an omnivorous reader, Frances Molloy began to write in 1980. *No Mate for the Magpie* is her first novel, a portrait of the artist as a young woman. About her beginnings as a writer she says, 'Mother Ireland may provide an uncomfortable bed for the childhood and adolescence of many of her writers, but what she scants in comforts and freedoms she richly compensates in the raw material later to be transmuted into fiction.' Ann Elizabeth McGlone is a memorable character – irreverent, seemingly luckless, a hoarder of experiences, and a wonderfully deceptive subversive.

Arella Weir
Portland, Or.
may 9, 1990

FOR GERARD, MARY
AND JOSEPH WITH
GRATITUDE AND
AFFECTION

The author wishes to express her thanks to Derek Noonan, for his kindness and much-valued criticism.

Chapter 1

Way a wee screwed up protestant face an' a head of black hair a was born, in a state of original sin. Me ma didn't like me, but who's te blame the poor woman, sure a didn't look like a catholic wain atall.

The state of original sin didn't last long. That's wan good thing about me ma, she maybe didn't like me but by god she done hir duty by me an' didn't lave me lyin' there in the clutches of the divil. That very day a was took te the chapel at the tap of the town be me godmother, that me ma didn't like either, an' hir husband who could have been me uncle if me ma hada married hes brother who was handsome an' beautiful an' iverythin' me da wasn't. But me ma, on a point of principle, jilted him, an' he went te England way a broken heart an' married an oul woman an' made a lot of money.

A was called after me two grannies, Ann, after the catholic wan, an' although me ma didn't like it much, Elizabeth, after the oul protestant wan, just for the sake of pase.

When they brought me home a was wrapped up nice an' snug an' put in a drawer. (Wee wains are safer in drawers than they are in cots, an' it's just as well too at

1

the price of cots.) A would have slept in me drawer till a grew outa it, which mighta took a long time (my family are not famous for growin'), if it hadn't been for the arrival on the scene of me wee brother. A was then took outa me drawer an' put inte a bed beside me big brother. He was better at not falling outa bed than a was so they put me in nixt te the wall. He was wan year ouler than me an' he peed the bed but he was nice. Even me ma liked him then. (She would probably have gone on likin' him if a priest hadn't prophesied when he was five that he would turn out te be a bad boy. A think it was for sayin' fart in school but a can't be sure, maybe it wasn't anythin' that serious, but whativer the reason me ma always expected the worst aff him after that.)

Wan day before me wee brother was born our house went on fire because me ma kept guinea-hens. Mine you, she had been well warned agen keeping them be people that knew the hazards attached te havin' these unfortunate fowl about the place but me ma was a bit of a sceptic in them days an' she recklessly disregarded all the warnin's she was give. Needless te say she has niver took any more risks of that kine since because if it hadn't been for the miraculous medals that me an' me big brother were wearin' at the time it mightn'd have been only the house that went up in smoke.

It happened at a time of the mornin' (eleven a-clock) when we were usually put inte bed for our middle of the day nap (wee wains need a rest in the daytime, it helps them te sleep at night). But that day didn't the miraculous medals make me an' me big brother kick up hell an' refuse te go te sleep or do a damned thing we were toul, so me ma took us out inte the yard te feed the livestock (nine bantam-hens — we had a dozen but ate three — six guinea-hens an' two turkeys).

When we made te go back inte the house again we foun' it was on fire so me ma had to run for help te me godmother who we weren't speakin' te at the time on account of the fact that she was our nearest neighbour an' it was most likely hir wains that were stealin' the gooseberries aff our bush wheniver me ma wasn't lookin' but ye have te overlook things like that in an emergency. .

Me godmother was great at handlin' calamities so she jumped on me godfather's bike an' headed aff for the fire station at the foot of the town shoutin', McGlone's is on fire, McGlone's is on fire, McGlone's is on fire, but be the time the fire brigade landed our house was burned te a cinder. We couldn't live in that house anymore so we had te be took in be relatives.

Me da went te live way hes own people an' me ma brought me an' me big brother te live way hir family. Me ma's own people used te niver speak te me ma because she married me da that they thought wasn't good enough for hir. (A do'no what they had agen him for as far as a can tell no illegitimate births were iver known of in hes family so they couldn't have thought that he was an oul low-come-down.)

Me ma's people forgiv' me ma for marryin' me da when word landed from the hospital that she was dead less than a year after the weddin'. It wasn't hir that was dead atall (the polisman that brought the message was drunk) but the wain she had who would have been me big brother if he hadn't of died three years before a was born. The nurse in the hospital that had christened him couldn't mine whether she had called him John or Patrick because she was busy an' got the two wains that had died that mornin' an' been christened be hir mixed up so me ma sometimes referred te him as wee Patrick an' sometimes as wee John just te make sure that she got hes name right half the time. All through the years when we used te let me ma down an' break hir heart way all our oul tom-foolery, she would cry an' say how things would of been wile different for hir if wee John or Patrick had of

3

lived an' not died because he was the best wain she iver had.

Livin' way me ma's people didn't work out for us because me big brother got inte a wardrobe an' leaped about inside it an' it fell an' got broke an' me ma's people blamed it on bad blood so me ma left them an' we all went te live way me da's people. They didn't have much room atall for they only had a wee house (me ma's people called it a cotter house) way two rooms in it. But me da's people knew about this other house that had a man just died in it so they made inquiries an' got it for us an' we went te live in it.

It had a long bumpy lane leadin' up te it. When we were movin' in me ma spied a ghost hunkered in behine a bush an' he was the spit an' image of the oul fella that had just died in the house. He must have been wonderin' what kine of a rare crowd we were because me doll had got burnt in the fire an' me ma couldn't afford te get me another wan so she gave me a statue of the Sacred Heart instead an' although it was as hard as the hobs of hell a was houlin' it wile tight an' clutchin' it te me chest an' the red van way the furniture in it that all the people from our town had chipped in an' bought for us an' got their names wrote in a wee blue book fornenst the amount they gave, was rockin' about like a boat in a storm an' me da shoutin' te the man that was drivin' it te whoe, like he was givin' directions te a horse.

Me ma was great at spottin' ghosts an' had even talked te wan at a party on an all-souls night when she was seventeen. Three other people seen that ghost too but only me ma spoke te it. She spotted it the minute she landed at the party an' said te hir sister (because it was a wile oul lookin' ghost), my god, they're here from the cradle te the crutch, would ye look at thon oul wan thoner, she must be ninety if she's a day.

Two hours later wheniver me ma was danced aff hir feet she went te get a chair an' the oul wan got up an' pointed at hir own seat. Me ma said te hir, a god, don't be givin' yer chair te me mother, but the oul wan said te me ma, it's all right dear, a'm goin' now te rest. Way that she headed inte the outshot at the back of the room where there was nothin' atall but a bed an' me ma allowed that she was goin' te lie down. Me ma then set on the chair an' said te the person beside hir, who was that oul doll? What oul doll are ye talkin' about? said the person. The oul doll that was sittin' here a minute ago, said me ma. Sure what are ye sayin', said the person, there was nobody sittin' there all night till you did. Ye'r talkin' through yer hat, said me ma te the person, sure a was talkin' te hir mesel' an' she has just gone in te lie down in the outshot this very minute. Then me ma took the person te the outshot te confirm hir story an' foun' nobody there an' that was the first time me ma knew that it was a ghost she was confabbin' way all along.

Me ma was very perturbed be all this so she went te a priest an' toul him the story. He toul me ma that she had been talkin' te wan of the souls outa purgatory who in hir lifetime hadn't spoke civilly te hir neighbour. He said that god had made hir stay in purgatory till such times as she made proper restitution for hir sins be speakin' te somebody. God, the priest said, had ordained that that ghost couldn't speak a word te a soul but had te wait aroun' for somebody te speak te it first because that was part of its punishment. He toul me ma that she had released the soul outa purgatory be speakin' te it an' that it went straight up te heaven the minute it went inte the outshot. Me ma was wile pleased way hirsel' for havin' done this an' she used te tell us all about it often, wheniver me da wasn't aroun'.

This new house of ours was haunted right enough even though it was niver confirmed be a priest. Anyway, me ma didn't worry too much about it because she knew the way te handle ghosts an' she taught us all how te do the same. Ye should say the rosary ivery night, for instance, if ye don't want them te do ye any harm an' ye should niver curse or swear or gossip about yer neighbours or speak ill of the dead in case the ghosts would hear ye.

Our ghost was an' oul man way a walkin' stick an' hob-nailed boots an' he come down kine of heavy on hes left foot. He visited us three nights a week because he had lived in that house for over fifty years way hes poor oul wife who was bedridden for a lifetime in the outshot since a wain she had had went wrong on hir. The wain, hir only wan, died, an' hir the creathure niver done a days good after it.

On the nights that our ghost was due te land, me ma always left food out for him an' built the fire up an' set hes own oul chair in front of it for him te sit on so he would feel at home. Even though he was a friendly kine of a ghost we niver took any liberties way him an' me ma warned me an' me big brother niver to forget to pray for him because people in heaven niver haunt, only the souls in purgatory.

Goin' te mass was the best possible thing a body could do for the souls in purgatory. The first time a went te mass a was nearly three. It was said be a priest that we had in our parish at that time called Father Dan, an' he was a great man. All the people used te love him on account of the fact that he niver toul them how they were goin' te burn in hell foriver an' iver because of their sins. Instead he taught them bigotry an' how te boycott protestant shops.

Hes attempts to get people te boycott protestant shops was unsuccessful because the protestant shops were cheaper than the catholic shops an' they had vans that could go out te the far-flung regions of the parish so as people who couldn't afford te go te our town could shop in the discomfort of their own homes.

This priest felt very aggrieved be the treatment meted out te the catholics of Northern Ireland be the

Stormont government. He tried te get the people te stan' up for themsel's an' even the balance a bit but the people were so downtrodden that they just shrugged their shoulders an' said what a quare good man he was an' thanked god for him an' carried on as usual.

Father Dan had a wile lot of problems way the bishop of Derry who took a final turn agen him wan twelfth of July when he tried te stap some orangemen takin' over our town. The Minister of Home Affairs of hes day, the late lamented W. W. B. Topping, toul the orangemen not te come near our town as he was feared it would cause civil strife if they did, but the orangemen, bein' a law unte themsel's, didn't heed a word he said an' they arrived in our town be the bus load.

Rumours reached them when they landed that they would get a hot reception if they set a foot on our street so not bein' very brave atall they didn't want te face gettin' kilt. They had a meetin' te see if they could fine any way outa their dilemma when a great idea occurred te them. There was a phone box beside the buses so wan of them went inte it an' phoned up another priest that was in our parish at the time. He was a very powerful man an' could strike a body down dead as soon as he would look at him. All the people used te hate him on account of the fact that he was foriver tellin' them how they would burn in hell foriver an' iver because of their sins. Well, te make a long story short, didn't the orangemen explain their delicate prediciment te him on the phone an' tell him how they wanted no trouble or bloodshed or the like anymore than he did, bein' the respectable responsible citizens that they were. Hes heart went out te their heartfelt plea te be allowed te march our town so he agreed te lead them up it an' headed down te meet them.

Before very long there was this orange procession

that was banned be Stormont steppin' up our town way a priest at the tap of it, headin' in the direction of Father Dan an' a hefty wee band of resolute parishioners who were determined te stap the intrusion way force if it be necessary — an' necessary it did in fact turn out te be.

Well, as a said before, the bishop of Derry took a final turn agen Father Dan after that day so he sent him away te a wile wee remote place in Donegal where hes parishioners were mostly made up of mountain sheep of the scrawniest kine imaginable. Father Dan died there three years later at the age of forty-seven from pneumonia an' malnutrition an' the orangemen have been marchin' our town annually iver since.

Me ma's people were great at havin' family reunions. When a was a wee wain a was always took te them. A don't know why they had these doos because they always ended in ructions. They would start aff paseably enough way me granny (the catholic wan), makin' wile big feeds of goose or turkey or somethin' like that an' iverybody sittin' down thegether te ate it on a Sunday.

People would smile an' be wile polite an' pass things but a used te be feared sittin' there for they always ended the same an' so a have niver been a great lover of food iver since. It was pass remarkin' that always started these fights at me granny's banquets.

It's too bad ye couldn't learn manners an' reach for the pratie nearest te ye instead of grabbin' the biggest wan on the plate, a visitin' aunt would say te wan of hir sister's wains. The wain's ma would then retort, too bad ye don't keep an eye on yer own brat, look at the pile of meat he has on that plate of his, it's enough to feed a ploughman. Before long people's wains would be called bastards an' plates would be flung.

Me granny, who was a pase lovin' woman, would try te calm things down but that always made matters worse. People would demand te know who's side she was on an' when she said she was on the side of the wains she would be accused of showin' favouritism. Then they would start te take all the skeletons outa the family closet an' even invent a wheen that weren't there atall.

A had this wan aunt way the unlikely name of Mercy, she had red hair an' was better at riotin' than the rest. When the worst things she could say would do no more damage te hir opponent, she would start heavin' the furniture about an' headin' out the door way it.

The stair carpet that she had purchased for hir ma would unfortunately be hel' in place be stair-rods that had been bought be a rival aunt. She would proceed te take up the carpet an' the aunt that owned the rods would threaten dire consequences if she didn't take hir hans aff hir property immediately. The two would hurl themselves at each other an' soon big tufts of hair would be yanked outa heads an' wicked nails, painted cartwheel red, would plough bloody drills in angry faces. Uncles would have te pull the pair apart an' they would go an' lock themsel's in separate rooms te huff all afternoon.

When things would quieten down me granny would get up way a wile sad lookin' face on hir an' try te put the house in order again. Then the wains of all the different aunts would go out inte me granny's garden te hurl stones an' abuse at each other till it was time te come in an' get ready for devotions in the chapel at six a-clock.

A was lucky a suppose te have a granny te visit atall because me protestant granny died when a was two year oul, just a wheen of months after we went te live in the house way the ghost in it.

It was discovered early on that a had a natural aptitude for washin' dishes, cleanin', cookin', nursin' bas an' changin' nappies so a wasn't sent te school at the usual age. Me ma knew hir catechism though. She knew that there were two kines of sin an' that

9

confession was needed te check actual sin wance a body reached the use of reason. Wan day it was decided that a had reached that state so me ma done hir duty again. Way the oul divil foriver lurkin' aroun' on the lookout for wayward wee souls she thought it better te take no risks so she sent me te school for a while.

The first thing the teacher taught me was mortal sins — sins of the flesh, stealin', lyin', cursin', cheatin' an' breakin' all the commandments. She taught me the commandments too but somehow a managed to grasp the sins better. A was no good at sins till a started school, but maybe that was because a didn't know any. Wance a got te know them though, it was hard te avoid them — especially sins of the flesh, touchin' the body — which was the biggest sin of them all.

A really did try, but it was hard — especially wheniver a had to go te the lavatory, but a managed all right for a while — then this itch started an' a had te scratch it. It would of done no good gettin' somebody else te scratch it for me because that was a sin as well.

A was lucky a suppose that a went te school atall an' had these sins pointed out te me because, just think, a could have been sittin' there at home in blissful ignorance, sinnin' away te me heart's content an' damnin' me soul te hell.

There were two teachers in our school, wan in the big room an' wan in the wee room. A went te the wan in the wee room. Hir name was Mrs Greene an' she was wile good at knittin'. She knit nearly all day — jumpers an' socks for the wains in hir class. (In a pinch she could even knit knickers, if there was any obvious need for them.)

Things would have been all right in hir class a suppose if it hadn't been for the fact that ivery wance in a while she went clean aff hir head an' ripped the jumpers aff us an' stuffed them inte the big open fire.

We would sit there shiverin' watchin' hir shovin' them well in way the poker.

Nixt minute she would be takin' the tongs te them an' draggin' them all out onte the hearth. As soon as they had cooled down a bit she would examine them anxiously te see what the damage was like. Then she would say, houlin' up the most presentable wan, this wan isn't too bad, is it? We would all say, naw mam, an' the lucky owner would come timidly forward te claim hes hot jumper. The nixt mornin' she would land in school way a big bale of wool, the best that money could buy, an' then she'd start te knit us more nice new jumpers.

They say she wasn't always like that an' that she was a fair nice kine of a woman in hir time, before hir daughter, a lovely girl it seems, got inte some kine of trouble an' had te go away te England, but that was before my time. Anyway, she only went mad about four times a year an' ye could get a fair enough bit of wear outa yer jumper between bouts if ye were lucky.

Another thing Mrs Greene was good at was readin' stories te us outa a book that she kept locked up in a cupboard along way hir handbag an' a cane. It was the only book in the wee room that wasn't about god an' although a couldn't read, a loved it. It was wrote be a man from America be the name of Joel Chandler Harris an' it was big an' dusty an' grey an' smelly. Ivery night a used te pray that she would give it te me but she niver.

The thing Mrs Greene was best at was catechism. She knew all the sins aff be heart an' she taught them te us ivery day. When a had been goin' te school for three weeks a made me first confession wan Friday mornin' in the wee room.

When it was my turn te go in a got the shock of me life because all the desks had been cleared inte a corner an' the priest was sittin' on a lonely chair in the middle of the room. The only thing a could think

about wheniver a seen him there was a song me ma
often sang te us about a poor wee croppy boy —

'Good men and true in this house who dwell
To a stranger bouchal I pray you tell,
Is the priest at home? or may he be seen?
I would like a word with Father Green.'

'The priest's at home boy, and may be seen.
'Tis easy speaking with Father Green.
But you must wait till I go and see
If the holy Father alone may be.'

The youth has entered an empty hall —
What a lonely sound has his light footfall,
In the gloomy chamber chill and bare
With a vested priest in a lonely chair.

The youth has knelt to tell his sins.
"Nomine Dei" the youth begins.
At "Mea Culpa" he beats his breast
And in broken murmurs he speaks the rest.

'At the siege of Ross did my father fall,
And at Gorey my loving brothers all.
I alone am left of my name and race.
I will go to Wexford to take their place.

'I cursed three times since last easter day
At mass time once I went to play.
I passed the churchyard one day in haste
And forgot to pray for my mother's rest.

'I bear no hate against living things
But I love my country above the king,
So Father bless me and let me go,
To die if god has ordained it so.'

The priest said naught, but a rustling noise
Made the youth look up in wild surprise.
The robes were off, and in scarlet there
Stood a yeoman captain with fiery glare.

12

With fiery glare and with fury hoarse,
Instead of a blessing he breathed a curse.
'Twas a good thought boy to come here and confess,
For one short hour is your time to live.

'On yonder river three tenders float,
The priest's in one if he isn't shot.
I hold this house for my lord the king
And, Amen, say I, may all traitors swing.'

At Geneva Barracks that young man died,
And at Passage they have his body laid.
Good people who live in peace and joy,
Say a prayer, shed a tear, for the croppy boy.

A stood in the doorway lookin' in an' me heart went
out te me poor ma an' da an' the shivers started runnin'
up an' down me back wheniver a thought about how
they ould grieve for me after a had died for lovin' me
country above the king.

The yeoman captain stood up an' come over te the
door an' took me be the han'. When he got back te the
chair he set down again an' lifted me up on te hes
knee. It was high. He said, you're Ann, aren't ye? A
said nothin'. He said, are ye not goin' te give oul
Father Devlin a smile Ann, an' he tickled me under the
chin. A didn't laugh. Then he started singin' to me —

Horsey, horsey, don't you stop,
Just let your feet go clippity clop.
Let your tail go swish,
Let your wheels go round,
Giddy up, we're homeward bound.

an' as he sung he bounced hes feet up an' down aff the
groun' like a horse gallopin'.

A took a wee look at hes face when he was singin'
an' he had big bushy black eyebrows way nice grey
happy dancin' eyes in underneath them. He didn't look
wan bit like a traitor that was about te breathe a curse
on me at any minute.

After he was finished singin' at me he said te me,

now pet do ye have any wee thing that ye want to tell me about? A forgot that he was a yeoman captain way fiery glare an' a started te tell him about the sins of the flesh that a had done.

He stapped bein' happy an' jolly then an' started gettin' wile cross. He said, god give me strength or wan day a'll swing for that oul bat. Then he toul me that a couldn't do sins of the flesh atall an' that the teacher wanted te be locked up in the big house for scarin' poor wee wains stiff an' if me bum iver got itchy again a was to give it a good scratch.

Then a toul him me other sin, lickin' sugar, an' he started te smile again an' after that he said some prayers at me in a foreign language. Then he lifted me down aff hes knee an' said, now Ann, a have te give ye some penance, what de ye think it should be? A thought about how me smallest sin crucified me saviour over an' over again so a said te him, a suppose ye'll be sendin' me te the Island. He started te laugh an' he said, naw pet, a'll not be sendin' ye there for in fact a have yer penance right here way me, an' he put hes han' in hes pocket an' took out a big bar of chocolate. Then he said, for yer penance, ate all this chocolate yersel' an' don't be givin' any of it away.

Wheniver a got out the door Mrs Greene was standin' way a row of other wains that were waitin' te go in an' then a minded that a hadn't done it the way she toul me te.

A should have gone in an' kneeled down an' blissed mesel' an' said, bliss me Father for a have sinned, an' a didn't. He should have said te me, how long is it since yer last confession, an' he didn't. Then a should have said, Father, this is my first confession, an' a didn't.

A started to worry that a hadn't been te confession right atall or even worse, that a had made a bad confession. Then a begin' thinkin' about what the priest had said about oul Mrs Greene needin' te be locked up an' a come te the conclusion that he musta been right. Sure didn't ivery body know that this was the first confession day — iverybody — me ma an' da an' me big brother an' all the neighbours — because it had been announced at the chapel on the Sunday before? An' wasn't it the priest himsel' that had announced it? So what would he be wantin' te ask me was it me first confession for wheniver he knew already? After a had finished comin' te me conclusion about the teacher a went out te the yard an' hid in behine a tree an' done me penance.

A only seen that priest about three times after that an' wan of them times he was dead. He was lyin' in hes coffin in the chapel an' iverybody had te walk by him an' touch hes han'. Outside the chapel door people were sayin' that he was lookin' very well an' ye could easily tell that he had gone straight up te heaven, but a didn't think that he looked well atall an' wheniver a touched hes han' a allowed that heaven musta been a quare coul place.

We had a new parish priest after that an' hes name was Father Curry. He was a wile saintly man an' he had the cure. He was a great believer in confession an' wile well up in sins. After he come te our parish, confessions took an awful lot longer than they used te do, but, like the people all said, he done a thorough job, an' ye always felt relieved when ye got out.

A wheen of months after he come te our parish some men burnt down the house of a bad woman an' she had te jump out the upstairs window te escape. When she was in hospital Father Curry went an' heard hir confession an' brought hir back inte the church again. The day after she got out of hospital she shot hirsel'. The say it was because she had repented of hir evil ways an' that god forgiv' hir (isn't god good?).

After a had made me first confession a had te lave school again because me ma had a wile lot of wains. Me brother that had took over me drawer was sleepin' in a bed beside me big brother an' another wee brother that hadn't been born at the time a slept way me big brother was sleepin' in the bed way them too. Be this time a was sleepin' in a bed be mesel' an' we had flitted te a new house in a place called 'Korea' because the neighbours were always fightin' an' throwin' bricks an' bottles through each others windows.

Before we moved away from the house way the ghost in it, a had a wee sister. Me da toul me that he had ordered hir specially for me be writin' a letter te god tellin' him te sen' me a sister because a had too many brothers. Me da was wile good at things like that — he even knew how te get our roosters te lay Easter eggs. Ivery Easter Sunday mornin' he used te waken us up wile early an' take us te the hen house where we would fine the chocolate eggs way the nice tinsel paper covers that only our roosters could lay.

He niver toul me at first that a had a wee sister on the day that she was born. He just come outa the house an' set down on me sunshine stone way a wee box in hes han' an' said te me, Ann pet, a got a wee present for ye, can ye guess what it is? A was standin' on tap of me sunshine stone houlin' on te me sunshine.

(My sunshine was a wee tree that wagged in the wind an' a always used te talk te it an' sing its wee song te it —
You are my sunshine, my only sunshine.
You make me happy when skies are grey.
You'll never know dear, how much I love you.
Please don't take my sunshine away.

A loved me wee sunshine an' a used te worry about it on stormy nights.)

The day me wee sister was born a wasn't singin' te me sunshine atall, a was cryin' te it because a was ashamed of mesel' for beatin' me doll called Jane that me ma an' da had bought for me because the oul hard statue used te give me big bumps in the bed.

A was in a bad mood wheniver me da come an' set

down on me sunshine stone an' asked me could a guess so a said te me da, naw. He said, come on now pet, just wan wee guess. A said, a doll. He said, naw, somethin' far nicer than that. A didn't know many things that were nicer than a doll so a thought for a long time an' then a said, a donkey. He said, naw, somethin' far nicer than that. If it had of been anybody other than me da a would have thought he was kiddin' me on because a didn't think there was nothin' in this worl' nicer than a donkey.

Well, when he toul me it was a wee sister that a had an' showed me the box she had come in, a jumped on him an' started te cry. A didn't know what a was cryin' about because a was happy, so me da toul me that a was cryin' way joy an' a believed him.

When we moved inte this new house in 'Korea' somebody give us a cot, so then me ma had a cot, two beds, an' a drawer for hir wains an' they were all full.

We were supposed te be wile lucky because we got this new council house in 'Korea' an' me ma was all delighted for a while bein' newfangled way the tap an' the scullery an' the three bedrooms an' the big windows an' two doors an' all that kinea stuff but after a while she started te regret goin' te live there atall.

Te begin' way, me godmother got a house in 'Korea' as well an' as soon as she moved in she got wile big way all the other weemen livin' there. But she was foriver fallin' out way them all an' havin' great big fights an' comin' complainin' te me ma about them. Me ma always advised hir the same, te keep away from the other weemen an' stay at home an' look after hir own wains but after the fights would cool down, me godmother would get big way all the neighbours again for a while.

(Me godmother wouldn't have been me godmother atall if a hadn't of been born in nineteen forty-seven, the year of the big snow. At the time a was born, we were snowed in, in the house that got burnt, an' me ma had te get me godmother te be me godmother on account of the fact that there was nobody else livin' near enough for hir te ask.)

Another reason why me ma had reservations about livin' in 'Korea' was that the neighbours were foriver knockin' on hir door an' askin' hir for things like milk an' sugar an' tay an' butter an' bread an' eggs an' flour an' paraffin oil for their lamps. If me ma had any of these things in the house she didn't like te refuse them in case their poor wains were starvin' way hunger in the dark so she always give them whativer she could.

After we were livin' in 'Korea' for a wheen of weeks people started te come te our house way shoppin' lists an' they didn't ask me ma could they borrow things no more but just said, a'll have a bit of this an' a bit of that. Soon me ma had te lock the door when she seen them comin' an' get us all te be quiet but they would bang an' hammer an' shout wile loud till me ma would have te go out an' tell them that she had nothin' te give them. They would go away screamin' an' swearin' abuse at me ma an' me ma would come in cryin' an' tell us that she didn't like te turn a poor soul away, only she didn't have enough money te pay for the goods that she got on tick from the shop belongin' te the man that always lit hes cigarettes way matches that he took outa boxes on hes shop shelves an' struck on the hip of hes trousers so as the people who were buyin' them wouldn't twig on that some of them were missin'.

Wan day me ma left me wee sister outside the house in 'Korea' in hir pram for a wheen of minutes an' the nixt time she went te look at hir the pram was empty. At first she thought that me da or me or me big brother had lifted hir outa hir pram but when she foun' out that we hadn't she got inte a terrible state an' started runnin' roun' the neighbours askin' them had they seen anybody takin' our wain away, an' they hadn't.

Me godmother, who was wile good at handlin' calami ties, jumped up on me godfather's bike an' rushed down te the town tellin' iverybody that our wain had been stole outa its pram outside our house an' had any of them bechance seen it?

Nixt door te us there was an oul widda woman livin' way hir three middle-aged daughters that had niver been married. They hadn't spoke te any of the neighbours since the mornin' they got up an' foun' a placard way a wile lot of rude stuff wrote on it, stickin' in the middle of their front garden. It was the day after wan of the daughters had got a nice wee letter published in the local paper that was called 'The Sixpenny Liar', about our new houses not havin' lavatories in them.

The first house me ma knocked on wheniver me wee sister went missin' was this house nixt door but wheniver they didn't answer the door me ma allowed that they musta been out. When me wee sister was missin' for nearly four hours, me ma an' da were goin' up the walls. Then they heard a wain's voice cryin' in nixt door so they run an' burst inte the house an' foun' me wee sister sittin' on wan of the oul dolls' knees. The rest of the oul maids were all sittin' roun' on chairs waitin' for their turn te nurse hir. Me poor wee sister was bawlin' hir head aff an' when she seen me ma she started te give wile big heavin' sobs an' then she put hir thumb in hir mouth an' fell asleep way hir head on me ma's breast because she was fatigued way all the cooin' that the four strange oul wans had been doin' at hir all afternoon.

Wan day word landed in 'Korea' that our breadman had cursed the pope. He was a protestant an' they say that he cursed the pope the night before in an' orange hall. A do'no how they could have known because only protestants went inte orange halls, an' none of them would hardly tell on him, even supposin' he did curse the pope.

But me godmother an' three other weemen outa 'Korea' knew all about it so they went an' set on the side of a ditch te wait on him the nixt time he was te come. They all went out at eight a-clock in the mornin' te wait even though the breadman niver come before twelve a-clock in the middle of the day. They set there all the time laughin' an' chattin' an' smokin' like they were sisters an' niver had a row way wan another ivery other day.

Wheniver the breadman landed they all smiled wile sweet at him an' waved even before he had time te get outa hes van. They all said, how are ye Bobby, it's a gran' day an' things like that. He got outa hes van nice an' friendly like he always was an' walked aroun' te the back an' said, good afternoon ladies, very proper te them, are ye all out enjoyin' the sun?

As soon as he opened the back of hes van they all changed an' jumped up aff the ditch an' grabbed a hoult of the things they were sittin' on an' charged at him way them. He nearly drapped down dead on the spot way the fright wheniver he seen me godmother runnin' at him way a pitchfork an' the other three behine hir, wan way a bill-hook, wan way a hatchet, an' the other wan way a pair of hedge clippers.

He run roun' the side of hes van an' jumped inte the driver's seat an' tried te make aff in a hurry but they were too quick for him. They all flew aroun' te the front just as he was startin' up but he couldn't drive forward in case he would flatten them. Then he started backin' but me godmother stuck the pitchfork through the front window an' the glass got broke an' cut hes han'. She jabbed the pitchfork at him te try te get him on the face but he juked te the side an' only wan prong hit him on the brow.

He tried te grab the pitchfork as the wan way the hatchet was climbin' up on te the tap of hes van an' the wan way the hedge clippers was screechin', way a wile mad lookin' look in hir eyes, te the other three te get him outa hes van for a wheen of minutes an' let hir at him so she could make him rue the day that he was iver born te an' oul orange fuckin' bitch.

Then there was a wile hue-an'-cry at the back of the van because some of the wains outa 'Korea' started pullin' at the cakes an' buns an' bread an' stuff an' begin' arguin' over who owned what. The nixt thing, didn't wan of the wains fine a box way money in it. As soon as me godmother an' the three other weemen heard about the money they stapped what they were doin' an' rushed aroun' te the back of the van te see if they could get any of it an' then the breadman drove away an' niver come back te 'Korea' again.

That night when we were supposed te be asleep, me ma an' da had a long chat. Me an' me big brother listened te them in behine the door. Me da asked me ma would she like us te lave 'Korea' an' me ma said she would but where would we go? Then me da said that he would look out for a place, for anywhere would be better than 'Korea'. Me ma said that the tap an' the sink an' the three bedrooms an' the big windows an' the two doors wasn't iverythin' an' sure what good was space te ye anyway wheniver ye couldn't let yer wains out te play for fear they would be mixin' way a whole crowd of oul low-come-downs?

Me da agreed an' said that if we got a nice wee place in the country be oursel's somewhere we would be far better off an' he could afford te do some renevatin' te some oul house now that he had got himsel' the job. Me ma said that if that was the case we would have no more bother way havin' our praties an' cabbage dug up on us in the middle of the night an' we wouldn't need te whitewash our turf an' coal ivery night because nobody would live near enough te steal them. Ma da said that he might even be able te get us a goat an' me ma allowed that that would be gran'.

Chapter 2

At the time me ma an' da got married me da had a quare good job. He brought me ma on hir honeymoon to Bundoran for a fortnight. Wheniver he got back aff hes honeymoon the man me da worked for had gone broke so after that me da kept puttin' in for jobs but he niver got wan till we went te live in 'Korea'.

It was a quare good job too because four hundred people put in for it. Me ma had a special prayer that she got us all te say wheniver me da went away lookin' for a job in hes good Sunday suit after she had sprinkled him way holy water te bring him good luck.

The day me da landed home way the job me ma seen him comin' out the window an' she knew he had got it before he come inte the house because of the way he was walkin' an' on account of the fact that he had only been left home a wee bit over an' hour, for if he hadn't of got it, she reckoned, he wouldn't have been rushin' home in such a hurry te tell us the bad news.

The first day he went te hes work me da landed home upset an' we were all sittin' roun' wile excited waitin' te hear how he got on. As soon as he got in he took me ma out inte the scullery way the sink an' the tap in it an' closed the door behine him. Me an' me big brother listened in behine the door but we wouldn't let the wains listen in case me da said somethin' that they shouldn't hear. Me da toul me ma that he'd had a wee bit of bother in the town wheniver he was doin' hes work. Me ma said, Sacred Heart, don't tell me that ye have gone away an' lost yer gran' good job on the very day ye started it.

Before me da got hes job, a farmer used te go about the town way a tractor an' collect all the rubbish that the people had an' then they would pay the farmer. Then the council made a rule of some kine that it was dangerous te health te let the farmer do it. The council toul the people that they were te get themsels things called dustbins way right good tight fittin' lids on them an put the rubbish, that they called refuse, inte them an' lave them outside their houses te be emptied be me da.

The council made some kine of rules for me da too — that he wasn't to be goin' inte people's yards if the dustbins weren't left out for him unless the people were oul an' infirm or pregnant way their husbands workin' away in England.

Well, the first day me da started work he done iverythin' the way he was toul. He went up the street an' emptied the bins that were left sittin' out an' went inte the yards of the people who were oul or infirm or pregnant way their husbands workin' away in England. He didn't go inte the yards of the people that didn't bother te put their bins out atall in case he would lose hes gran' job that he had just got.

He was about te get inte hes lorry te take it back te the depot wheniver he heard a wile hullaballo down in the middle of the main street that was the only street in our town. A man that owned a shop that sold dear clothes, a wile big important high-up man that always carried the canopy at the chapel wheniver the Blessed Sacrament was bein' brought up an' down the aisle be the priest, rushed out inte the middle of the street trailin' hes dustbin. All the other people in our town come out te watch. He started shoutin' abuse at me da sayin' that the likes of me da were bein' paid good ratepayers' money te serve the public an' he wasn't wan bit satisfied way the way me da was servin' him.

He said it was a disgrace that people didn't know the meanin' of the word serve anymore an' that he for wan wasn't goin' te stan' for it. Then he started te empty all the rubbish that he had been savin' since the time the council made the rule about health, out inte the middle of the road.

After me da had toul me ma all about this they opened the scullery door again an' come back inte the kitchen. Me ma had me da's dinner ready for him but he said he didn't feel like aten a bite but me ma made him ate because there was no point in lettin' good food go te waste.

Wheniver me da was halfway through hes dinner a knock come te our door. It was a wile big important high-up man from the council. He come in an' shaked han's way me ma an' da an' patted us all on the heads. Me da said that we were te all go down te the room for a wheen of minutes te let him talk te the man, an' we went, but me an' me big brother listened in behine the door.

The man from the council said that he had got a complaint an' that he had investigated the complaint an' foun' that me da was in no way te blame for the incident. He said it was unfortunate that this thing had happened an' he said that he was sorry te me da. Then he asked me da te go down the town te lift up the rubbish.

Me da said he wasn't gettin' paid te do a thing like that way all the people in our town standin' aroun' lookin' at him an' the man that put the rubbish there would be better te clean it up himsel'. The man from the council toul me da that he had already been te see the man from the shop an' he had refused te clean it up so it would be very helpful of me da indeed if he was te do it as a favour. Then the man from the council took out hes wallet an' give me da some money te do the favour an' me da said he wouldn't do it in the broad light of day but maybe he would go an' do it first thing in the mornin' before anybody else was up.

The man from the council thanked me da an' then he shaked han's way me ma an' da again an' then he went away. Wheniver me da got te our town the nixt mornin' at six a-clock te clean up the rubbish, it was gone an' nobody iver foun' out who done it.

Because me da got this quare gran' job we were all able te lave 'Korea'. The house we moved inte was the same size as the wan way the ghost in it but the man that owned it said me da had hes full permission te renevate it.

Before we moved in me da done a lot of improvements. He made a nice new floor in the kitchen an' put on a new door an' made the windows bigger. After we started livin' there he carried on way the renevatin' ivery evenin' as soon as he come home from hes work. He was makin' two bedrooms upstairs in the laft, way a trap-door in the ceilin' so me ma would have plenty of room for all hir wains. There was a mile long lane leadin' up te our new house from the road an' it was great because nobody could come aroun' bangin' on yer door askin' ye for food wheniver ye didn't have any.

We were livin' in this new house an' gettin' on gran' when somethin' awful happened te us an' we were niver the same after it. We just went te our beds wan night an' we were sleepin' away like we always done wheniver this wile noise wakened us all up. Even though it was the middle of the night it was as bright as day outside an' we thought it was the en' of the worl'.

We didn't have time te get our clothes on before the door of our new house was broke down an' dozens of

25

polismen an' 'B' specials rushed in an pointed guns at us. All the wains begin to cry. The 'B' men started rippin' our house apart lookin' for somethin'. They pulled up me da's new floor an' went up inte the laft an' smashed up the two new rooms. They ripped up the mattress on me ma's an' da's bed an' pulled out the stuffin' an' threw it on the floor. They done the same te our two beds an' the cot that somebody give me ma wheniver we went te live in 'Korea'.

There was a hell of a din on outside an' all roun' our house there were bright spotlights an' rows of 'B' men pointin' guns at us. Some of them went inte the out-house that we kept our goat called Bessy in an' Bessy got scared an' started te run away but some of them run after hir an' caught hir an' begin te kick hir. She started te pee an' they all laughed at hir.

Then they poured me ma's drum of paraffin oil out onte the yard an' peed on the four-stone bag of flour that me da was payin' aff for at a shillin' a week. Then they beat me da up an' broke hes teeth an' kicked him out the door an' threw him inte the back of a van an' toul him that they were goin' te do wile bad things te me ma an' us. Then they drove aff way me da way them an' they niver toul us where they were takin' him.

Me da was away from home for two weeks before me ma heard anymore about him. Wan day two ordinary polismen come te our house way guns in their belts an' said te me ma, send on yer husband's underclothin'. Me ma then allowed that me da must be in jail so she sent hes underclothin' te the Crumlin Road in Belfast.

A wheen of days after that me ma got a card from me da sayin' that she was te go te see him. Well, me ma headed aff te the Crumlin Road jail te see me da an' when she got there he toul hir that he couldn't get out because they were tryin' te get him te sign an' incriminatin' document sayin' that he would have nothin' more te do way the I.R.A. an' he couldn't do that because it would be the same as admittin' that he had been havin' somethin' te do way them when he hadn't.

Me ma toul me da that he was doin' the right thing an' there was no need for him te be signin' any incriminatin' documents. When she come home she toul us all what incriminatin' documents were an' we all agreed that she had give me da the right advice. Me da didn't sign the document so they kept him there for four years an' we all set about at home plannin' ways for him te escape.

Wheniver me da was in jail me ma had a lot of trouble. Te begin way, she had hardly any money because me da wasn't at home te work or get us anythin' te ate. Me ma had niver been the best han' at makin' money in the worl' because she was always far too busy lookin' after all hir wains. In the en' she had te apply te the authorities for national assistance an' the authorities sent people out te our house te quiz me ma. Me ma wasn't too used te bein' quizzed be anybody an' she didn't like the authorities very much because they were the same authorities that put me da in jail.

Well, they quizzed hir a lot, all about us an' why a wasn't goin' te school an' was a ill an' things that were silly because a had niver had anythin' wrong way me, only the flu wance an' impetigo. After they had finished quizzin' me ma the authorities toul hir that she wasn't fit te look after all hir wains (eight) way me da away in jail. They said they would take all hir wains away from hir if she didn't get me da te come home an' help hir.

Then they started te sen' health visitors out te me ma te quiz hir about me wee brother that was niver able te walk or talk. She said, niver ye's mine about him, but they pretended te be wile concerned about him allthegether an' toul me ma so.

Me ma got feared then an' toul them how me wee brother had had a very difficult birth. She niver let on that the doctor who would have been a priest if he hadn't left the seminary the night before he was te be ordained, wasn't at the birth in the back room of our house in 'Korea' even though he got me ma te sign a paper the nixt day sayin' that he was so as he could get paid for bein' there. Or that the midwife who had han's that were blessed be the pope had panicked when me wee brother was born not able to breathe, an' knelt down beside me ma's bed an' took a special prayer that she kept for all emergencies outa hir han'bag an' started te read it out loud an' get me ma te read it after hir, before she went about makin' me wee brother breathe.

Instead me ma toul them that she was quite capable of lookin' after all hir wains an' that she had done it all anyway even before me da went inte jail. They said that she was clearly not able te cope on hir own because she had always te keep me at home from school te help hir. Me ma toul them that the oul school was no good anyway an' that a could learn a lot more from bein' at home way hir but they wouldn't believe hir.

Me ma then went up te the Crumlin Road jail an' toul me da all that had been goin' on. She said that they were tryin' te break hir an' him down way their oul devious ways but that he had no need te worry because she would stan' by him an' support him in ivery way. When she come back she toul us all about our da an' how he was losin' all hes hair an' gettin' wile oul lookin' an' we all started te cry. In the long run, when all was said an' done, the authorities won because me ma had te put me wee brother inte a hospital an' sen' me back te school.

Wheniver a went te school again a had te go inte the big room te the other teacher who was the headmistress of our school. She wasn't married way a beautiful daughter that could break hir heart be gettin' inte any kine of trouble like Mrs Greene but she musta had troubles of hir own the poor soul because she used te sit on hir desk lookin' inte space talkin' te hirsel' way a smile on hir face.

All the big boys in the school were in hir class an' she was sometimes wile shockin' scared of them allthegether. If she tried te stap them from fightin' or tearin' up books or stickin' pins in girls or drinkin' the milk that was meant te be shared be iverybody or takin' the sheep dung outa their pockets te flick it at people from the en's of their rulers or rippin' up other wains' coats they would go up an' stan' in a ring roun' hir starin' at hir way wile evil lookin' faces on them an' they would shove hir way their shoulders if she even dared te say a word.

There was only wan ordinary boy in our school who wasn't goin' in for the eleven plus that could read an' that was me big brother. He just learned te read all be himsel' because he liked readin' an' me ma kept a copy of *Wuthering Heights* in the house on account of the fact that she thought it was a quare good book. Me big brother could read anythin' that was wrote though, even if it wasn't in *Wuthering Heights*.

Ivery time the teacher went out for a walk or went visitin' the neighbours te complain te them about us, all the wains would shout at me big brother te gone an' read them a story. He would go an' get a book an' then sit cross-legged like a wee leprechaun on tap of the teacher's desk readin' te them. He was wile good at it an' even the big boys used te sit quiet listenin' because he made funny faces an' flung hes arms about an' acted all the parts that were wrote in the book when he was readin'. The wains were often far better behaved wheniver the teacher was outa the room than they were when she was in it.

Two times ivery year our teacher went away te have nervous breakdowns. Wheniver she was gone we always got men teachers in hir place te try te get the big boys under control for hir te come back te. Some of the men teachers were big gaelic footballers that used te batter the big boys about like they were nothin' more than punchbags. The big boys were sò feared of the big gaelic footballers that they had te get their mas te land at the school way big sticks te beat the livin' day lights outa the big gaelic footballers.

The other kine of men teachers that come te our school wheniver our teacher was away havin' hir nervous breakdowns were nice refined clerical students way wile clean white wee han's an' black suits that rid bicycles. They tried te explain te the big boys what was the proper an' right an' nice way te behave towards others an' especially towards our teacher who was a woman just like the big boys own mammies, but the big boys didn't pass any remarks on anythin' the clerical students taught them on account of the fact that they were happy enough way the way that they were.

Ivery time our teacher come back te us after havin' wan of hir nervous breakdowns she was a changed woman. She would stan' up at the front of the class like she owned it, shoutin' at people te come out at wance an' stan' in the corner way the dunces cap on them for not listenin' te hir. She didn't even seem te be feared of the big boys an' she niver went for walks or te visit people an' complain about us. When we all got impetigo she took it as a personal insult te hirsel' an' beat the scabs aff the backs of our legs way a big stick.

The other trouble that me ma had wheniver me da was in jail was neighbours. We had te flit te another house wheniver me da was in jail for a year because me ma was feared livin' on hir own way a whole houseful of wains in a wile remote place without a man, where she niver seen a soul for weeks, only the authorities, so she put in for a house down near the town an' got it.

The talk about this house was that it was gran' an' ye could turn on a light at the touch of a button an' that in no time atall the council would be puttin' in flush lavatories an' maybe even baths.

Anyway, the trouble started way the neighbours the minute we landed at the new house way all our things on the back of a tractor. The house was an oul kine of a house that was built long before the second worl' war. It had a big garden at the back an' a wee garden at the front an' three other houses of the same kine beside it an' wan that was different. The wan that was different had been specially built be the council for a district nurse but she had died so hir son lived in it then way hes wife an' family an' they were the only protestants about there.

The man that was drivin' the tractor had started te back it in the gate of our new house wheniver the neighbour on the left han' side of us come out an' shouted te him, mine where ye'r goin, if ye knock down my gate post ye'll have te pay for it. He said, niver you mine me, Missis, a know what a'm doin'. The neighbour shouted, a just hope ye do, but the man that was drivin' the tractor was wile good at it for he got it in backways way just wan inch te spare on either side.

After we got all our stuff inside me ma made the man way the tractor tay an' we all went explorin' the house. There were lights in ivery room an' ye didn't even need te put oil in them.

We were explorin' away when a terrible hullabaloo started outside. Me an' me big brother opened the upstairs window an' looked out an' seen the two weemen that lived in the houses on either side of ours, standin' out talkin' te each other. Only they weren't talkin' ordinary but shoutin', like they thought they were makin' speeches, about how they didn't like te be livin' near the likes of us an' how me da was a jailbird an' all sorts of stuff like that.

Me an' me big brother run down the stairs an' said te me ma, ma, them weemen are sayin' wile bad things

31

about me da an' us. Me ma said te us, niver ye's mine what themins are sayin', sure that's the kinea behaviour ye would expect from a crowd of oul hibernians. Ignore them an' come an' help me te get this house ready in case they let yer da out, we can't have him comin' inte a place like a pigsty after bein' away in jail all this time. Then we forgot about the neighbours for a while but the neighbours didn't forget about us.

Ivery time we come out the door, they come out too an' shouted somethin' rude at us, like the time me ma went out to clip the hedge an' the woman that lived on the right han' side of us opened up hir window an' said, Be careful not te clip my side, Maggie. Me ma said, don't worry, Sarah, a'm only trimmin' a wee bit aff me own side because it's growin' inte me garden too much, then the woman said, get yer man outa jail, Maggie. Me ma said nothin' but kept on clippin' till she was finished an' then she come in an' set down on a chair an' started te cry te hirsel' because she was sorry that she had flitted.

The woman that lived in the other catholic house was called Prudence. She stood outside hir gate all day ivery day stappin' people that passed on the road te try te start a wee chat way them. Prudence was married te an alcaholic called the Pontiff because he had a roman nose an' niver went to mass. Prudence had been a protestant when she was young but she turned te be a catholic at the time she married the Pontiff an' hir own people niver spoke te hir after that.

The four sons that Prudence an' the Pontiff had grew up an' left home niver te return again because they didn't want anybody te know that the Pontiff was their da. The only frien' that Prudence had in the en' was a dog called Peter that the Pontiff kicked ivery time he landed home drunk. Peter run away from home a wheen of times after these kickin's an' Prudence had a lot of trouble gettin' him te come back again.

Wan day she solved the problem be gettin' a big post an' drivin' it inte the middle of hir back garden an' tiein' Peter te it at the en' of a wile long tether. He strained an' tugged an' whimpered for the first day or so an' after that he stapped an' set te mopin' for a while. Ivery body toul Prudence that he was sure te die, but he didn't. He just stood up wan day an' started walkin' roun' an' roun' the post at the extremity of hes tether. It sickened him a bit te begin way but he niver stapped an' in no time atall he had a nice wee path made for himsel' way the constant walkin'. For the first week or so of circlin' the post he kept on goin' in the same direction but after he got used te it he musta decided te give himsel' a wee bit of variety for he started countin' the times he walked an' ivery time he done seven clean circles he stapped an' turned an' done seven more roun' in the opposite direction.

Me an' me big brother watched him from our upstairs window waitin' for him te escape because me ma wouldn't let us cut him loose on account of the fact that it was none of our business what the neighbours done way their dogs an' Prudence was a good soul an' fed him ivery day.

When Peter was tied te hes post for two years wan day hes tether broke an' a went an' called me big brother an' him an' me went up the stairs eight steps at a time te see Peter runnin' away, but he was still walkin' roun' in circles, seven times wan way an' seven times the other way hes poor oul head turned out the way it always was an' the tether trailin' limply along behine.

As soon as Sarah's wains an' the wains of the woman that lived on the left han' side of us heard the news about Peter they all landed on Prudence's garden te get a quare oul laugh at Peter walkin' roun' an' they jeered an' kicked at him in the way the 'B' men had done te our goat Bessie the time they come te lift me da. Peter niver tried te bite them or even bark but he just kept walkin' aroun' till Prudence come out way a big stick an' chased them all away. Prudence niver needed te tie Peter up again after that because he just kept on walkin' seven times in wan direction an' seven times in the other till wan day he died an' Prudence pulled up the post an' dug a hole where it had been an' Peter got buried in a nice roun' grave.

Well, they were the three catholic neighbours that me ma had in hir new house but she niver had any trouble way Prudence like the kine she had from the other two. She had no trouble way the protestant woman that lived in the bungalow either.

Wan day when we were livin' in our new house for a week an' the weemen on either side of us had been shoutin' ivery time me ma an' us went out, the wee protestant woman come an' knocked on our door. Me ma brought hir in an' made hir a cup a tay an' she said that she hoped me ma liked hir new house. Me ma said it was gran', then the wee woman said she hoped she wasn't talkin' outa turn because she was a protestant an' me ma said not atall.

The wee woman said that she didn't think a lot of the way some of the other neighbours were treatin' me ma but me ma wasn't te worry because if iver she was in need of anythin', anythin' atall, she knew where te come, an' me ma said, o aie, a know right enough. Then the wee woman asked me ma how me da was doin' in the jail an' me ma said, gran' an' the wee woman stood up an' shaked han's way me ma an' wished hir ivery luck in hir new house.

The two weemen that lived on either side of us made loud speeches about the kinea people our family were consortin' way wheniver the wee woman was goin' out our gate but me ma toul us that she was a quare good wee soul an' we believed hir.

A wheen of days after we moved inte our new house me an' me big brother climbed up inte the laft. It was crammed full of stuff so we come down an' toul me ma that we had foun' treasure. She said it wasn't treasure atall but some things that belonged te the people who had lived in our house before we did an' they musta stored them away an' forgot about them. Me ma toul us te bring it all down so she could give it back te the people.

It took us a wile long time te get all the things down. Me ma put them in a box an' when the box was full she went an' give it te the man that had lived in our house before us an' toul him that there was still more te come yet an' she was wile nice te the man about it. The man was wile curt way me ma an' she said when she got home that ye would think he didn't want the things back atall an' it all good stuff like clocks an' lamps an' candlesticks an' vases. She said it was wile odd.

The last thing me an' me big brother brought down te me ma was a whole big pile of letters that we foun' in a box because it took us a wile long time te read them all way the wee dim light of a flashlamp for the battery was nearly flat.

The letters were wrote be the man that had lived in our house before us te hes wife an' be hes wife te him. They were all wile rare letters an' te begin' way we could make neither head nor tail outa them.

In some of the letters they would be sayin' how they loved each other more than anythin' else in the worl' an' how they would niver stap thankin' god that they had had the good fortune te meet each other because ivery body else in the worl' was a whole lot of oul rubbish an' things like that. The letters all had dates an' the address of our new house at the taps of them which was the silliest thing of all because they both musta knew rightly where the other wan lived.

The nixt day after they had swore that they loved each other they would be writin' about how they hated each other an' sayin' if they knew what was good for themsel's they wouldn't go te sleep at night or they might niver wake up in the mornin'.

She said that he would need te watch what he was aten in case it was poisoned an' that the nixt time he come at hir way a hatchet she would have him locked up in the big house for iver an' iver. Then after a wheen of days they would start tryin' te pretend that it was all somebody elses fault an' that they were blessed an' lucky te have each other because all the other people in the worl' were nothin' more than a whole lot of rubbish.

Before we brought the letters down te me ma, after we had read them all three times, me an' me big brother had a discussion about them because we thought we were on te a murder plot. We were sure that wan of them was goin' te get done in but we weren't sure whether he would kill hir way a hatchet or trip hir up at the tap of the stairs or smother hir way a pillow or be the wan te get knocked aff himsel' way the poison.

Me big brother said that we would have te fine the motive first. A said that he likely married hir for hir money an' now that he had got it he maybe wanted rid of hir. Me big brother toul me that people who lived in council houses didn't have any money so it couldn't be that. He thought it more likely that hir face was so ugly he couldn't bear lookin' at it ivery day for the rest of hes life.

The nixt Sunday when me an' me big brother went te mass we went an' set up in the seat beside the man an' hes wife an' had a quare good look inte hir face an' sure enough it was very ugly indeed so we both agreed that the motive was foun'. Then a set te thinkin' that if the man hada thought hir face was ugly he would niver have married hir in the first place but me big brother said that maybe he had te. A said a thought people married who iver they liked but me big brother toul me that wasn't always the case but a was too young te understand an' he would explain it te me nixt year after he foun' out more about it himsel'.

We both agreed finally that we had foun' the motive — he couldn't stick the ugliness of hir face an' it would be hir that would get done in. Then we had another discussion te see if we could stap the murder. A said that the best thing would be te tell me ma. Me big brother said that that wouldn't be such a good idea atall because me ma would fine out that we had been pokin' our noses inte other people's business. A toul me big brother that a life depended on it. He said, ye better watch out that me ma doesn't kill us. A said that she wouldn't because she would think we were heroes for savin' a life.

So we toul me ma that we had foun' out about a murder plot after readin' some letters an' that the murder was goin' te happen soon unless we put a stap te it. We toul hir te read the letters for hirsel' so she could see how serious it was but she said, a'll do no such thing. She beat me an' me big brother an' said what a show we made of hir in front of the man that used te live in our house. She said that, that explained te hir why the poor creathure had been so distant wheniver she called te deliver the stuff he left in the laft. He musta thought she was readin' their letters when she was doin' nothin' of the kine. Me ma then threw all the letters inte the fire an' sent me an' me big brother te bed without our supper an' we have niver stuck our noses inte other people's business since.

Wheniver we moved te the new house me ma had te sen' us te another school. She went te talk te the headmaster of that school an' he toul hir that me big brother was of bad rearin' an' that he was reluctant te have him in hes school atall because of the bad report the headmistress way the nervous breakdowns had give him. He said he would take him only outa charity because he was a good livin' christian man an' me big brother was a child of god even though he was a bad wan. He said he would teach manners an' breedin' te me big brother an' he'd take no nonsense from the likes of him, a troublemaker.

He niver said anythin' bad about me or me wee brothers or sisters so a didn't expect any trouble wheniver a went te the new school the first day. A was too feared te talk all the same so the teacher shouted at me an' called me a cheeky brat because me voice wasn't workin'. A tried te answer hir a couple of times but it was no good so she come down an' hit me on the face an' that only made me cry. Then she made me stan' in a corner an' toul me that she didn't have any cheeky wains in hir class but she was tellin' me lies because some of the wains stuck pins in me an' others said, ha, ha, your oul da is in jail. She only clapped hir han's at them an' said, now come, come children, pay attention.

A was in the new school for about a week wheniver the teacher took a quare shine te me. She started te call me Ann dear an' tried te turn me inte the teacher's pet. That put me inte a terrible state of bewilderment an' te this day a have niver been able te trust a body that changes wile aisey. Te make a long story short, didn't she decide that a was a great singer on me ma's side of the family an' that a should come te a wile big do of a party for the choir that she was havin' in the Commercial Hotel in our town.

She was the head of the choir in the chapel an' had played the organ since the time she was jilted be a man she was courtin' for ten years. A said a would ask me ma an' a did an' me ma went te a shop where she could get tick an' bought me a gran' new outfit. She taught me a wee song te sing as well because she allowed that ivery body would have te do their bit on account of the big feed.

Wheniver a landed at the party all the gentry of the town were at it. Even the man that had emptied hes rubbish in the middle of the street because me da wasn't servin' him right an' the priest that had led the orange men up our town the time Father Dan was in the parish. He was jumpin' about tryin' te pretend te iverybody that he was a wain an' gettin' them all te laugh at him because he thought it was wile smart te burst people's balloons way hes cigarette lighter.

A wanted te take my balloon home for me wee brothers an' sisters te play way an' after a had been at the party for about an hour, my balloon was the only wan left. A kept it safe in underneath the table between me knees so he couldn't get at it an' a set there aten way a wile plain lookin' look on me face so as nobody would twig on.

He was sittin' up at the tap of the table talkin' away nice an' friendly te some other big bug. Then he pretended that he had drapped hes fork or somethin' an' when he went in underneath the table te get it the first thing a knew was me balloon burstin' an' a cheer risin' up. He come out from under the table an' stood on hes chair an' hel' hes han's up in the air like he was after performin' some wile great miracle. Then iverybody shouted, three cheers for Father John, like he was a hero or somethin'.

Well, a have niver went te many parties since then because all the people at that party were clappin' each other on the backs an' sayin' how it was that the choir parties were the best parties iver, an' a suppose they musta knew well what they were talkin' about because they were the kine of people that went te an awful lot of parties.

After we had been livin' in the new house for a while, the two weemen that lived on either side of us were fairly hoarse because no matter how loud they shouted we niver let on we heard them. Even if them or their wains come out te jeer us wheniver we were emptyin' our lavatory bucket in the hole in our garden. They musta forgot that they needed te do things like that themsel's.

Wan time word landed from the school that me wee sister mightn't get makin' hir first confession because hir baptismal certificate got lost be the teacher at the oul school. The two weemen made a lot of speeches about that, shoutin' across te wan another that me wee sister wasn't baptised atall an' it was most likely because she was the daughter of some oul tramp aff the street or maybe even oul Nick himsel' an' we couldn't get any dasent priest te put holy water near hir.

Me ma warned us that if iver we evened our wits te the likes of the two of them be answerin' anythin' they said, we would be as bad as them oursel's, an' she said if we ignored them long enough they were bound te get fed up talkin' te the walls, an' she was right because after a wheen of months they got tired makin' speeches an' stapped. Then me ma started te get these anonymous letters that weren't even signed be the people that sent them.

The letters scared me ma stiff because they said she would better lave our new house an' things like that or else she would be sorry. They sent me ma wile bad things that were called contraceptives that they said she needed te stap hersel' havin' any more wains.

Me ma cried an' took the letters an' things called contraceptives te the priest that burst my balloon at the party an' toul him that she was feared te sleep in hir bed at night in case any of the threats were carried out an' she asked him what she should do. He toul me ma that the people that done things like that were obviously sick an' he couldn't guarantee that they wouldn't try te harm me ma an' us, an' hes advice te hir would be te go te the polis. Me me toul him that she didn't think a lot of the polis since the time they put me da in jail.

Then he said that the only other thing he could think of doin' would be te mention it in the strongest possible terms in hes sermon on the nixt Sunday mornin' in the hope that the people responsible would be listenin' an' get feared an' stap. Then he toul me ma te go home an' pray for the people that had done it.

Wheniver me ma come home from the priest she toul us what he said an' she got us all te pray for the people too because wains' prayers are stronger than grown-ups' prayers on account of the fact that wains is innocent. Then me ma toul us that anonymous letters were wile evil things an' she asked us te promise that we would niver sen' wan te anybody, even our worst enemy an' we promised.

After the priest made the speech in the chapel about the evils of some people behavin' in an unchristian way towards their neighbours an' how they would all burn in hell for iver an' iver because some sins were just too bad for god te forgiv', like writin' anonymous letters te people that were tryin' te bring up their wains under difficult enough circumstances, an' mockin' the laws of nature be sendin' unholy articles through the post te people, the anonymous letters stapped an' things started te go wile smooth for us, even though me da was still in jail.

Wan day Sarah's daughter started te get wile big way me at the school an' she said that a could walk a bit of the way home way hir because she really liked me even though she couldn't show it in case hir ma murdered hir. A started te go aroun' way hir an' like hir but wheniver wan of hir brothers or sisters come along an' seen us talkin' she started te pretend that she wasn't me frien' atall but that she hated me.

A felt sorry for hir an' a went about way hir for a while but wan day a got fed up an' toul hir what a thought. That she was yalla, an' a didn't think that no yalla person was a good frien' for anybody te have an' if she wanted te be my frien' she was just goin' te have te stap bein' yalla, but she niver so then a stapped goin' aroun' way hir.

After that a started gettin' friendly way the wee

protestant woman's daughter. Hir name was June an' she was the best fun te be way because she wasn't always goin' on about how iverythin' was a sin like all the other girls a had iver been pals way before. She niver even mentioned sins, even if she seen yer knickers wheniver ye were climbin' up a tree or paddlin' in the bourn.

A was wile big way June for a wheen of months wheniver the strangest thing happened. She started gettin' an oul nose on hir comin' up te the twelfth of July but it didn't last long an' soon we were as good frien's as iver.

Wheniver the nixt twelfth of July was comin' up a started te worry that maybe June was yalla too just like Sarah's daughter, so a said te hir, a suppose ye'll be havin' another oul nose on ye at the twelfth this year? She said she didn't have no oul nose on at the twelfth of July an' that it was me that had the oul nose on. A said that it wasn't, an' she said, it didn't matter wan way or the other just for a wheen of days because protestants an' catholics niver spoke te each other at the twelfth.

Well, a toul hir that they should, an' she allowed that a was right so then we made a great plan te stap protestants an' catholics fightin' on the twelfth of July wheniver the orange marches were on an' at the fifteenth of August wheniver the hibernians were marchin'. A said that a would go way June on the twelfth of July an' march along beside hir in the orange parade an' wheniver iverybody seen what a great idea it was they would all folly suit.

June said that she would do the same thing way me on the fifteenth of August, but a toul hir that a didn't go te marches on the fifteenth because a was not a hibernian but just an' ordinary person. She said it wouldn't be fair for hir te get me te march when she couldn't do the same for me, but a toul hir that be the time the fifteenth come aroun' that year, protestants an' catholics would be out marchin' thegether anyway, because of our example.

We were both wile excited comin' up te the twelfth but we had te keep our plans a secret in case anybody foun' out an' tried te stap them. That year the twelfth was a wile nice sunny day. A tried te slip out without me ma seein' me, but she spotted me headin' out in me good frock that she had got for me te go te the party in the Commercial Hotel, an' asked me where a was goin'. A was about te tell hir the truth but a changed me mine wheniver a thought of the face me ma would have on hir if a said a was goin' te an orange march, so a toul hir that a was goin' te the chapel te say a wheen of prayers an' she said that was a good idea an' a was te pray that the marches in the town would pass aff paseably.

Wheniver a got te the town it was full of 'B' men an' polismen walkin' about way guns. All the houses in the town had their curtains closed an' some of them had their holy pictures an' statues an' crucifixes standin' up in the windows lookin' out wonderin' what was goin' on. A got te the bottom of the town an' all the orangemen were ready te march. There were crowds an' crowds of people that a had niver seen in me life before. A was about te go home again wheniver a heard June shoutin' te me. She was wile happy an' delighted te see me because she thought a musta changed me mine or got caught.

We headed up the town an' there was a wile shockin' lot of noise allthegether. First there were the ban's way their big drums beatin', then there were people cheerin' an' clappin' in the crowd behine the ban's, an' drunk men singin' orange songs outa tune. There were some people in their houses that opened their upstairs windows. Some of them were sayin' the rosary wile loud, others were singin' 'Faith Of Our Father's' or 'Full In The Pantin' Heart of Rome', some were dippin' holy palms that had come especially from

43

the holy lan' for palm Sunday, inte big basin fulls of holy water an' shakin' them at the orangemen. Others were swearin' an' cursin', an' wan of the weemen outa 'Korea' that had attacked the breadman way me godmother, was standin' on the steps of hir mother-in-law's cafe pullin' up hir skirts te show hir bare arse te the orangemen an' the holy statues standin' lookin' out.

A walked wile close te June's ma because a was wile feared an' she put hir arm aroun' me an' give me a whole lot of biscuits an' chocolates an' sweets. Wheniver the march was over a went home, wile shockin' proud a mesel' allthegether, thinkin' that a had put a stap te all the squabblin' that went on aroun' the twelfth between protestants an' catholics but a hadn't. It didn't do no good atall. Even me ma laughed when a toul hir. She said it musta been the orange blood that a got from me protestant granny that made me go out in answer te the call of the Lambeg drums.

Chapter 3

Wheniver me da was in jail, me ma an' us listened te the news ivery mornin' at eight a-clock te hear if he was let out because if any of the internees were released, it always give their names on the news. Wan day a heard that me pen pal was let out an' a was wile happy. A had been writin' te me pen pal for years since the time a taught mesel' te read an' write after me da got lifted so as a could write him letters te the jail. It took me only about five minutes te learn te read me ma's book, *Wuthering Heights* because a knew the A.B.C.'s since the day Mrs Greene wrote them on the blackboard for an inspector comin', but a had a lot of trouble teachin' mesel' writin' because it was wile hard te get the letters te sit on the paper the way they were in me head.

Me da was in jail for nearly three months before a was able te write te him an' be that time he wasn't called me da atall but number 535, internee. Anyway, me da wrote back te me a gran' long letter tellin' me all about this wee boy from the Bogside who was in the jail way him since before he was age for lavin' school. Me da toul me that the wee boy was pinin' away for hes ma an' that hes da wasn't long dead an' that he didn't have a lot of frien's in the jail an' him only a

wheen of years ouler than me big brother an' me. Me
da said it would be great if a could write an odd letter
te him, so a did, two times a week for three years.

Me pen pal was a great scholar allthegether an' had
been doin' well at school till the night the 'B' men
landed at hes house te arrest hes big brother. They
couldn't fine hes brother anywhere so they took him
instead just outa spite. They were thinkin' they could
get him te tell where hes big brother was a suppose,
an' then te sign himsel' out, but he niver.

He wrote me the greatest longest letters of the day
tellin' me about the things me da was doin' an' what it
was like te be livin' in the jail. It wasn't very nice atall
because some of the other internees kept teasin' him
all the time for bein' young an' sayin' hes prayers ivery
night an' for not signin' himsel' out. Wan of them
chased him roun' the yard way a penknife iverytime he
went out for exercise, pretendin' that he was goin' te
cut hes throat, an' if it wasn't for me da, he wouldn't
know what to do.

There was another internee that they kept teasin'
too, not because he was young but because he was the
only protestant in the jail. Ivery time the priest come
te the jail te hear confessions, they grabbed the
protestant internee an' made him sit in the queue till
it was his turn an' then they shoved him inte the
confessional box an' closed the door behine him tight
so as he couldn't get out, just for the oul laugh. An'
on Sunday mornin's they always trailed him along te
mass way them an' stuck his head inte a bucket of holy
water that was sittin' at the door. In the en' the
protestant internee had te sign himsel' out agen hes
principles because they wouldn't give him no pase.

Me pen pal always toul me in hes letters that the
minute he was released, he would rush straight home
to see hes ma an' then get the first bus he could catch
an' come te visit me an' me ma an' me big brother an'
all the wains because we were the best frien's he iver

had. When he was outa jail for a wheen of weeks a thought he had forgot about me because he niver come te see me atall. Then word landed from the jail about how he wasn't keepin' very well. It seems he got a disease that had a wile big name.

On the mornin' we heard about him gettin' out on the news, some screws landed in hes cell an' called out hes number an' toul him te pack hes bags an' go to the governor's office. That was when he took this disease an' had to lie down on hes bed. He stayed there for three days an' then some doctors come an' looked at him an' said there was nothin' the matter atall.

Wheniver the screws come in again an' toul him te go te the governor's office, he just lay where he was. When the screws grabbed him he hel' on tight te hes bed but they were stronger than he was so they got him up an' put hes things in a case an' pulled him along te the governor's office. After the governor was finished way me pen pal the screws trailed him te the door an' threw him an' hes suitcase outa the jail inte the middle of the Crumlin Road. He didn't walk away. He just stood at the door knockin' an' kickin' an' pleadin' te get in. Then the polis came an' put him in a van an' brought him te the mental. That was why he didn't come te see me. The name of the disease that me pen pal got in the jail was institutionalisation.

A wheen of months after that we were all sittin' listenin' te the news in the mornin' as usual when low-an'-behold, didn't it say that me da was a thirty-eight-year-oul man from our town an' that he was bein' let outa jail that day. We all started te cheer an' clap an' dance aroun' the house an' up an' down the stairs, then we burst outa the house inte the garden an' outa the gate inte the road shoutin', hurrah, hurrah, daddy's comin' home the day.

It took me ma nearly half an hour gettin' us all rounded up in time for school. Wheniver we landed at the school that day there was wile excitement. All the wains were shoutin' an' sayin' that our town was mentioned on the wireless an' me da's name was read out on the news. They were fightin' away way each other te see which of them could get sittin' beside wan of us. Even the wains that stuck pins in me wheniver a started at the school. They musta thought that we were film stars or somethin'.

At lunchtime the teachers let all the wains have a free afternoon in case me da would pass by the school. They got the wains te comb their hair an' stan' up nice an' straight an' practise shoutin' allthegether, welcome home Mr McGlone. Ivery time anybody walked up or down the road all the wains would crane their necks an' say te us, there he is, there he is, even if they knew that it was only the milkman.

When a woman that went past the school ivery day te go te the protestant school down the road te breast-feed hir son who was a wee bit simple like hes ma went by they said te us, is that yer da? Then some of them started te shout te hir, welcome home Mr McGlone. She come over te the wire way the same wee half smile that she always had on hir face an' started to explain' te them that she wasn't Mr McGlone atall.

They laughed an' jeered at hir an' said the wile bad things that they had learned from listenin' te their own das talkin' te their frien's outside the chapel after eleven a-clock mass on a Sunday mornin', only not as loud as they usually done in case the teachers would hear them.

She said that Mr McGlone was a wile big name an' she had heard about him on the news but they were mistaken in thinkin' that she was him because she was just an ordinary woman an' would niver be important enough te be on the news. She said that she knew Mr McGlone. Then wan of the teachers shouted te hir te be aff way hir an' she run away at a wee half-trot lookin' back scared.

Well, we stood outside the school all day waitin' for me da but he niver landed. A begin te worry maybe he had got the disease me pen pal took an' been carted away be the polis te the big house. That evenin' when we got home from school me ma had the house lookin' like a wee palace an' all the gran' things she had baked for me da's tay were sittin' coolin' down in the scullery.

In the time me da was in jail we used te often cry an' lament about havin' no da te set on people that give us a bad time but me ma always toul us that we should think of the poor souls that had no das or had das that were dead an' would niver come back te them, instead of mopin' an' feelin' sorry for oursel's when we knew rightly that if we waited long enough our da would land home wan day. Well, even on the day that our da was let outa the jail we didn't believe hir right till nearly seven a-clock in the evenin' when didn't this Land Rover pull up at the en' of our road an' a man got out an' waved te the driver an' come headin' over in the direction of our house.

Sacred Heart, me ma said, it's him, an' we all started te run te meet him. A was the first te get near him an' he drapped hes suitcase in the middle of the road an' come runnin' up te me way hes arms out sayin', it's my wee Ann. A stapped just in time an' stood back quick because a could see that it wasn't me da atall but a wee wizen oul lookin' man way a bald head, pretendin' that he knew me very well.

A was standin' there lookin' at him when didn't me ma an' all the rest of them land. Him an' me ma started huggin' an' kissin' each other an' cryin'. Then the two of them started walkin' back in the direction of our house way their arms roun' each other.

Hundreds of people started te land in our house te shake han's way me ma an' this strange wee man that iverybody thought was me da. It wasn't very long before there was a party goin' on way people wile

49

happy an' clappin' each other on the backs. Only the wee man was lookin' uncomfortable an' a allowed that it was because he was feared that somebody might find out that he was an imposter.

A decided that a would have te have a wile serious talk way me ma, but a had a lot of trouble gettin' a word in edgeways way hir because of the big do that was goin' on. A had niver seen me ma lookin' so happy in hir life before an' a didn't like te be the wan to spoil it on hir an' hir nicely dressed up in the gran' frock that she had made hirsel' te wear in case they iver let me da out.

A knew that sooner or later the truth was bound te come out an' that the earlier it was settled the better so a got me ma te the wan side an' a said te hir, ma, a have some bad news for ye. She didn't even notice the serious mood a was in so she just said te me, what is it? That's not me da ye'r makin' all this fuss about, a said, that's a sheeoge.

A what? me ma said, laughin'. A sheeoge, a said, a wee changeling — can't ye see what's happened, ma, the fairies have took me real da away an' left that wee wizen sheeoge here in hes place? Me da was a lot bigger than that.

Nonsense, me ma said te me, he's the same size that he's always been, he might appear smaller te you because ye've got bigger yersel' in the past four years. A said, if that's the case why don't you look smaller te me too? A, she said, that's only because ye have been lookin' at me ivery day.

Of course a had expected that me ma wouldn't believe me because a knew that the nearest an' dearest was always the last te twig on wheniver the beloved was switched for a changeling. A wasn't convinced be what she toul me atall so as the days went by a watched him very closely for any other signs that would confirm me suspicion.

He would sit lookin' inte the fire for hours at a time,

niver speakin' a word te a soul. He niver went outa the house for two months. That was incriminatin'. But on the other han', he wasn't constantly grumblin', moanin', an' complainin', an' he didn't seem te be aten me poor ma outa house an' home.

A was at sixes an' sevens te know what te think when wan day the problem solved itsel' for me. He was sittin' beside the fire lookin' inte it as usual when an' oul frien' of me da's called in an' started talkin' to him. A wasn't listenin' all that keen because they were goin' on about somethin' strange that a knew nothin' about called the trade union movement. After a while the two of them started te argue away in the way men do about all kines of rare things that has nothin' te do way anythin' only who knows most, when somethin' he said made me ears prick up.

If that's what ye believe, then Tam, he said, all a have te say te ye is this, ye know as much about the English working class as my arse knows about shootin' rabbits. A knew that minute that me ma had been right all along because if me da iver disagreed badly way anybody, he ended up accusin' them of havin' about as little notion of what they were talkin' about as his arse had about shootin' rabbits. A looked at him again an' me heart went out te him as a realised at last, that this strange, wee, wizen, bald-headed, oul lookin' man was indeed me very own da.

Wan of the first things me da done wheniver he got outa the jail was write a letter te the council tellin' them that he had been absent from hes work for four years through no fault of hes own an' now that he was back he was prepared te take up hes employment again. Me da's job hadn't been officially filled when he was in jail because the man that worked way me da on the lorry brought hes own son te work way him the day he heard that me da was lifted, for, as he said te me ma at the time, it's a bad wind that doesn't blow somebody good.

In hes letter me da explained te the council that if they had give the job te another man in the same circumstances as himsel' way a wife an' a family te support, he wouldn't be wantin' it back. But as the man that was doin' the job was single an' livin' at home way hes parents an' hes father in full employment he thought it fair te ask for hes job back.

After me da wrote the letter te the council, he watched for the postman ivery mornin' before sittin' down te look inte the fire for hours on en'. Wan day a letter landed for him from the council. It said that the other man had put in for the job officially the day me da got outa jail an' there was te be a special meetin' of the council te decide who the job should go te on the followin' Tuesday fortnight at eleven a-clock.

When me da landed at the meetin' he toul the council that he understood the other man's feelin's in wantin' te houl on te the job because of the wile high unemployment but that the other man was in a far better position to fine work outside the area than he was because the other man didn't have a wife an' family te support.

The other man toul the council that he should keep the job himsel' because he had been doin' it for four years, three years longer than me da, an' that he was a respectable citizen way no blemish on hes character, not like me da who was a jail-bird.

After both sides were heard the Unionist council toul me da an' the other man te lave so that they could discuss the matter in private among themsel's.

Five minutes later they were both called back in an' the chairman of the council said that a decision had been reached an' that it was a very aisey decision in favour of me da. Well, me da went back te work an' was gettin' on gran' after a wheen of weeks when wan day he lifted up a dustbin that was sittin' out for him an' he nearly got kilt because it was full of nothin' but bricks way some wee bits of rubbish sittin' on the tap te make it look ordinary.

When me da was rushed te the hospital te have an' operation the other man tried te get hes job back again but the council wouldn't have him. Six months later wheniver me da went back te hes work he had te start way a new man because the father of the man that done me da's job when he was in jail got sacked.

The new binman was called Willie an' he was nearly as famous as me da because even though he'd niver had hes name read out on the wireless, he had a daughter that had got her photo in *The Coleraine Chronicle* as Colleen of the week.

After me da got outa jail we had no more need te spen' our time plannin' ways for him te escape so instead we started plans te make me ma rich an' buy hir all kines of mod-cons te do hir work for hir. Our first plan was te rent a field aff a farmer an' plant praties in it an' then sell the praties an' buy me ma a washin' machine. This plan fell through for nobody would rent a field te us because we were only wains.

Then we decided to go in for fishin' an' we went te the bourn late wan evenin' an' emptied a bucket of lime inte a hole full of trout. We loaded the trout inte a wheelbarrow an' ran home wile quick before the lime reached the town in case anybody seen it an' toul the polis. Me ma an' da foun' out about this an' put a stap te our plan te sell the trout te rich people te raise money so we had te ate them ivery day for breakfast, dinner an' supper. That put a stap to our fishin'.

We give up tryin' te get rich for a while after that till me wee brother, the wan that took over me drawer, got a great idea. He decided that we should go in for breedin' pigs so we built a pigsty out of all the oul bits of wood an' corrigated iron we could fine an' went te all the farmers of the day te ask them te give the nixt wee runt they got te us instead of drownin' it.

Me wee brother got three pet pigs on the wan day an' we had te feed them way a wain's bottle. We called them Janie, Sarah, an' Molly Mucreen an' be the en' of the week Molly Mucreen was the only wan left because Janie an' Sarah died. Te begin way me ma was out a fortune buyin' extra milk, an' coal te keep the fire on all night, but soon Molly Mucreen was big enough te lave hir cardboard box beside the range an' go outside inte hir pig-sty.

Wheniver she was a wheen of weeks oul me ma threatened te get rid of hir for she was aten us outa house an' home but me wee brother wouldn't part way hir atall because he dreamed of a day when Molly Mucreen would be the matriarch of a huge pig empire that would put all our troubles an' cares behine us foriver.

Roun' that time there was a protestant school built near our house way a gran' canteen te make dinners for the wains. Me wee brother went along an' asked the weemen that worked there what they done way all the food that was left over from the dinners. They toul him that it was put inte a slop bin that got emptied ivery day. He asked them if he could have some of the slops te feed hes pet pig an' they said he would need te ask the headmaster. Me wee brother come home an' washed hes face an' combed hes hair an' went back te the school an' the headmaster said, surely, so Molly Mucreen became the best fed pig in the country.

In no time atall she was as big as two sows an' all the wains used to ride about on hir back like she was a horse. Wan day me ma an' da said that Molly Mucreen should go te be serviced an' we all wanted te go too an' watch but me ma wouldn't let us. That evenin' Molly Mucreen was taken aff on the back of a tractor an' stayed away all night. The nixt day she come back an' the farmer toul us that she would have pigs be a certin date so we fed hir twice or three times as much as iver.

Me ma an' da set up way Molly Mucreen the night she was supposed to be havin' hir litter but nothin' happened so they had te sit up way hir a second night too. After that they got tired so me big brother set up way hir the third night an' me an' me wee brother the fourth. Be the en' of the week me ma an' da were so worried about poor Molly Mucreen that they sent for the vet. She was lyin' on hir side, pantin' an' groanin' an' puffin', as if she was about te breathe hir last breath.

Wheniver we toul the vet that Molly Mucreen had been in labour for a week he said that he had niver heard of the like before an' he rushed out te where Molly Mucreen was lyin' in the throes of agony an' started to examine hir. Then he toul us that Molly wasn't pregnant atall. He said it was because she was far too fat that she wasn't able to move. Me ma an' da then decided that we couldn't keep Molly Mucreen any longer so they sent hir away te be slaughtered an' me wee brother has niver ate bacon since.

That was the en' of our attempts te make money for me ma till me big brother was fifteen. The first thing he done the day he left school was get himsel' a job in a quarry as a labourer for fourteen poun' a week. Me da put a stap te that as well be tellin' me big brother that he would have te serve hes time te a trade for five years so he would niver have te become a binman or go on the dole or emigrate to England te get work.

The attendance officer was always callin' at our house te get me ma te sen' me te school. Ivery time he landed, me ma hid in the back room an' sent me te the door. Me an' him become very big an' we used te go for walks thegether te talk about what was the best thing te do about my education. Wan day when a was fourteen he wrote me ma a letter tellin' hir that if she didn't sen' me te school she would fine hersel' in court. The nixt mornin' me ma sent me back te school even though a hadn't been there for so long that me name was no longer on the register. The headmaster beat me an' toul me that a had a cheek on me for just comin' in an' sittin' down in hes school an' me not even on the roll.

It wasn't long after that till a was fifteen an' oul enough te lave school officially, an' a was glad that nobody could threaten me way the law any more like a was some kine of a criminal. Me ma an' da then decided that a should go te work in a factory about twenty miles away, where they made men's pyjamas an' dressin' gowns, because the money was great if ye were any good.

There was great talk about what a quare place the factory was an' how ye could make a fortune an' be drivin' about in a big swanky car after bein' there for a wheen of years. The day a was sent for the interview there was this nice man called the personnel officer that asked me a lot of questions an' things like what me hobbies were an' why a wanted te work in the factory. A toul him what me hobbies were an' that a wanted te work in the factory because me ma an' da heard that there was gran' money te be made. He asked me what age a was an' could he see me birth certificate an' a showed it te him. Then he patted me on the head an' said that if a wanted the job a was te come on the followin' Monday mornin' at nine a-clock an' the wages was two poun' six an' nine pence, an' if a iver had any problems a was te come an' see him an' a said a would.

The followin' Monday mornin' a turned up an' a was sick for a'm no good at travelin in buses. A woman called a supervisor took me te a big room way a wile lot of noise in it an' toul me that it was the machine room an' a was te learn te be a machinist. Then she took me te an' office an' toul me that a had te get fitted for an overall. A girl way wile nice perfume an' make-up on come an' asked me what size a was an' a said a didn't know. She asked me what size of bra a took an' a said a didn't wear a bra. Then she made a tired sort of face an' said, a suppose a'll just have te

56

measure ye, an' she begin' te pull out drawers an' push them in again like they were hir mortal enemies.

She got a tape measure out an' started te measure me, first roun' the waist. She said a was wile thin. Nixt she measured me hips an' said, oom, a suppose it'll have te be small woman. Then she measured me chest an' just laughed an' went an' got an overall an' give it te the supervisor an' said, it'll have te be shortened but that's your problem, an' they both laughed.

The supervisor took me te a machine an' toul me that if a was te learn how te work it the first thing a should know was how te switch it on. That didn't take long so then she showed me how te thread it an' how te work the pedals. After a while when a got the hang of it, it was great fun seein' the rows of sewin' bein' done without any trouble atall an' a allowed that me ma could fairly do way a sewin' machine.

The first real job a done in the factory was turn up the hem of me overall an' the supervisor said a done a quare good job for a beginner. Wheniver it was dinner time she took me te a canteen an' toul me that a could buy me dinner for ten shillin's a week if a wanted te. A toul hir that a had sandwiches so she said a could sit at any table a liked. A went an' set down at an empty table an' as soon as a started te ate, five ouler girls come over an' stood aroun' just lookin' at me.

Wan of them said, are you a catholic or a protestant? A said nothin'. Another of them took a cigarette lighter outa hir pocket an' lit it an' hel' the flame close te me face an' said, we only allow catholics te sit at this table. A got up an' walked away an' set at another table. They all follied after me an' kept on askin' was a catholic or protestant? In the en' a said a was a christian. Then the wan way the cigarette lighter said, we know you're a prod. A said, if ye know so much why de ye waste yer breath askin' questions? She lit the lighter again an' set fire te the side of me hair.

A screamed an' beat the flames out way me han's. Then a woman from our town seen all the hullabaloo an' come over te see what was goin' on.

The girls said a was a prod but she said, what nonsense an' toul them who a was. Then all the girls said they were sorry but they were sure a would understan' that a body couldn't be too careful. They asked me what a thought of the factory an' a said it was gran'. Then they toul me that a should come te a hop way them that night because the hops were great an' all the lovely fellas of the day would be there but a said a would be goin' home.

After a had finished aten a asked the woman from our town te tell me where the lavatory was an' she showed me. When a got there a nearly passed out way the cloud of thick smoke that hit me on the face as soon as a opened the door. Inside there were twenty lavatories all in a row down wan side an' twenty han' basins in a row down the other side. Girls an' weemen were sittin' on tap of all the han' basins smokin', or combin' their hair, or puttin' on makeup. All the lavatory doors were closed an' the loudest laughin' an' wailin' an' thumpin' an' screechin' was goin' on in behine them.

A walked up the full length of the room an' seen that none of them was empty so a stood an' waited in a corner for somebody te come out because a was in a hurry. A was standin' there for a long time for as soon as a door opened an' the people inside come out, a whole rush of new wans would burst in before me.

The bell went for the en' of dinnertime before a got a chance te go an' a was just puttin' the bolt in when two weemen come an' shoved the door in me face. Wan of them said, hey you, what de ye think ye'r doin' in the ladies toilets, an' a said a had to go. She said, ye have a cheek goin' te the ladies toilets an' you a wee fella, so a toul hir that a was a girl. Then they both grabbed me an' started to rub their han's all over

58

me chest an' say, ye'r not a girl, ye'r a wee fella. A started te cry an' tell them te lave me alone but they hel' on te me an' started te pull me knickers down. A took a bite outa wan of them an' she thumped me on the face an' made me nose bleed an' said a had no fun in me atall an' couldn't take a joke. Then they both went away an' left me alone.

A was workin' in the factory for nearly a year wheniver me ma went inte hospital te have another wain. Me da toul me that a was te lave the factory for a while te look after the wains till me ma was better. Me ma was in hospital for about a week when she had another daughter. That was the last wain me ma iver had.

As soon as the wain was born there was some wile talk about who the new godparents would be. All the aunts of the day were thinkin' it was their turn te be asked. Then me an' me big brother had a great idea allthegether te solve me ma's problem about which of them te pick. We went up te the hospital an' set on the side of me ma's bed an' toul hir she was lookin' poorly. She said she wasn't feelin' all that well atall. Then we toul hir that the last thing she needed wheniver she come home from hospital was a whole big session about which of the aunts should be godmother an' she agreed. We said we had a plan te save hir all the trouble of havin' te decide.

We toul hir that as it was too much of a responsibility te place on a person in hir frail state we would therefore volunteer te do the job oursel's. Me ma said that that wouldn't be legal. We said that it would, an' seein' that it was all right way the law an' me ma, it was all right way us, so it was settled.

Me an' me big brother went home an' made arrangements way the priest te have our wee sister christened the minute she landed home from hospital on the followin' Wednesday afternoon at three a-clock. At half-past three on the Wednesday the priest come te

59

our house te see why we didn't turn up an' we said that the wain hadn't arrived yet. He said that that was all right way him an' we could bring hir along as soon as she landed. At eight a-clock that night the priest come te our house again an' we toul him the same story.

He said, niver mine, if she lands at twelve a-clock the night just bring hir down an' a'll be there. It was nine a clock at night when hir an' me ma landed home from hospital an' me an' me big brother toul me ma about the arrangements we had made way the priest. Me da toul hir not te worry because he would go te the chapel way us himsel' te see that the wain was all right.

Me an' me big brother rebelled an' toul me da that he had let other people less capable than us go te the chapel way a new born wain many a time. We mentioned me godmother as an example an' said that if he thought we were no better able te look after an infant than hir, then it was a sad reflection on the way he thought our ma had brought us up. Me da then said that he had great confidence in the two of us allthegether. He walked way us out as far as the gate where the car was waitin' an' warned us not te bump the wain's head inte anythin' because wee wains heads are saft an' very aisley damaged.

Half way te the chapel me an' me big brother toul the car driver te stap as there was no hurry as far as the priest was concerned. Then the two of us started te confab about what we thought of the name me ma had picked for our wee sister. Neither of us thought too much of it an' te clinch matters there was a tombstone in the graveyard behine our chapel way the name Martha McGlone carved on it. We allowed that we'd have te think of a better name quick before we landed at the chapel where the harm would be done for good an' all.

When we settled for a name we were both agreed about, we toul the driver te move on. Then we thought of a good reason why we couldn't use the name so we toul the driver te stap again. Marilyn Monroe McGlone had a lovely ring te it allthegether an' Marilyn Monroe was aisely the most beautiful woman in the worl' accordin' te anybody that had eyes in their heads — anybody that is, except me ma.

That left us way the problem of pickin' a name that me ma would approve of. We tried te think of catholic film stars but couldn't come up way wan that was beautiful enough te call our wee sister after. A asked me big brother what he thought of the woman that was married te President Kennedy in America because a knew that me ma liked hir. Me big brother, who be this time was a great expert on beautiful weemen, said that Jacqueline Kennedy had the kine of a face that only a mother could love, an' that she would have te be a very, very broken-hearted mother too at that.

We were sittin' in the car along the side of the road way the wee ba on me knee screwin' its wee face up inte all kines of comical shapes that would have led me ma if she had of been there te say that it was seein' angels. The driver was moanin' an' complainin' about us takin' all night, so we had te hurry up an' decide quick. In the en' we minded about an' aunt we had who was a nun in Africa. She had a name that even me ma would approve of so we decided te call the wain Dania an' headed on, delighted way our choice.

As we come close te the chapel the two of us started te worry that maybe me ma would have a blue fit wheniver she foun' out that we hadn't called the wain after hir sister Martha like she said we should so we decided that we would be as well te give hir Martha as a second name just in case. When we were goin' up the chapel steps a said te me big brother, de ye not think that Dania Martha McGlone sounds like it has somethin' missin', an' me big brother allowed that a was right. Then a come up way a great idea te please me ma. Hir an' me da were both born on the feast of

St Francis of Assisi, the fourth of October, so a said te me big brother that we should call the wee wain Dania Martha Frances, an' he agreed.

When we brought the wee ba home from the chapel me ma an' da were delighted to see the three of us — especially the wain. Me ma said te me the minute a walked in the door, give me wee Martha now te a feed hir. A said te me ma that she wasn't called wee Martha. Me ma said, what de ye mean, she isn't called wee Martha? Me an' me big brother said te me ma that we didn't think no wee wain would like te sit up in its pram wan day an' realise that it had a name like Martha so we called hir a right nice kine of a name instead.

Well, we were right, me ma did have a blue fit. She said that niver in hir born days did she iver hear such cheek. Godparents goin' away an' pickin' a different name for a wain te the wan the parents wanted. Me an' me big brother huffed an' decided that seein' as me ma was so nasty about it we would get our own back on hir be niver lettin' on what the wain was called an' keepin' it a secret only for oursel's.

We toul hir that wheniver godparents landed home from the chapel way a newly christened wain they always got a big feed an' we asked hir what had happened te the gran' spread that we had set out on the table for oursel's before we left the house. She toul us that it had been give te visitors. Me an' me big brother were hoppin' mad an' we toul me ma that there would be a blue moon in the sky before we would iver stan' for a wain of hirs again an' me ma agreed.

For the rest of that night an' most of the nixt day me an' me big brother niver spoke a civil word te me ma an' da so they had te call the ba, the wee wain, because they didn't know who she was. Then me ma threatened te sen' for the priest so we relented an' toul hir, an' she took te it so well that in the en' she come roun' te believin' that the name was hir idea all along.

Chapter 4

Wheniver me wee sister was a wheen of weeks oul me ma an' da started te talk about sendin' me back te the factory again but as luck would have it a got bad way me throat an' the doctor said a would have te go inte hospital te have me tonsils took out. The hospital was down near the depot where me da's lorry stayed at night so on the day that a was te go inte hospital me da took me way him on hes way te work. When we landed at the hospital it was far too early for me te be admitted so a had te go aroun' way me da an' Willie collectin' bins for a couple of hours first.

We come back te the hospital way the suitcase in the middle of the mornin' an' me da was cryin' away because he thought he would niver see me again. Willie toul me da that he had nothin' te worry about because the Colleen of the week had been in te have hir tonsils out when she was three an' she had been as right as rain in a couple of days. Me da said it was a fairly aisey job takin' the tonsils outa a wee wain but that it was a different story allthegether when a body was sixteen.

The doctors an' nurses toul me da that it was a very simple operation that only took five minutes an' they asked him if a was all right otherwise an' he said a was gran'. As soon as me da an' Willie left, the nurses put me te bed in a ward way two other people in it.

Wan of the two was a girl of nineteen called Josie. The other was an' oul woman of over sixty that was after havin' a major operation an' couldn't get outa the bed. Josie was in hospital te have hir tonsils out too an' she had a boyfrien' that come in te see hir ivery time the nurses had their backs turned. She toul me that she was gettin' married the nixt year an' that she planned te have nineteen wains. A toul hir that if she done that she would have hir han's full.

The oul woman in the other bed was a wile shockin' plague allthegether. She niver stapped complainin' atall. Nobody could iver manage te please hir. The bed wasn't good enough for hir. The food wasn't good enough for hir. The doctors weren't good enough for hir. The nurses weren't good enough for hir. The woman that cleaned the ward wasn't good enough for hir. Me an' Josie weren't good enough for hir. Hir own family wasn't good enough for hir. In fact the whole bloody worl' was quite outa line way all hir high needs an' expectations. A niver met a wan like hir before in all me life.

The day before the operation she didn't bother me an' Josie all that much because when she started te moan we just went outa the ward an' sat in the bathroom way the door closed so we wouldn't hear hir grumblin'. On the night before the operation a priest landed inte the ward te hear the confessions of me an' Josie just te make sure that if perchance we died of the tonsils the two of us wouldn't have te live in hell foriver an' iver burnin'.

Wheniver he had finished hearin' the general confessions (Josie's lasted longer than mine because she had a boyfrien'), the wee man, outa ordinary common civility an' consideration for dasent good manners an' christian charity, went over te say hello te the oul wan in the corner. Now if she had anythin' the matter way hir that kept hir in the bed it wasn't the toxic tongue of hir. Niver in me born days before had a heard such an explosion of unprovoked abuse as that oul wan tellin' him what she thought of effin popish scum.

If there was anythin' in the worl' that the oul doll hated more than popish scum it was the black doctor that done the operation on hir te save hir life. Ivery time he come inte the ward she begin te screech even before he landed at hir bed. She kept sayin' how disgustin' it was that things like him were iver allowed outa the jungle an' that he should be taken away an' locked up in a zoo.

As a woke up from me operation the first thought that entered me head was that a musta made a terrible mistake way me general confession an' died an' landed up in hell after all. A was racked way pain from head te foot an' a could hear the voice of the oul divil himsel' deavin' me. The nixt thing a knew a was openin' me eyes an' seein' a wee nurse lookin' at me. She put hir arm roun' me an' toul me not te worry because she would stay beside me. In a wheen of minutes a realised that a was in bed in hospital an' it wasn't the divil who was deavin' me but the oul wan in the bed in the corner.

A didn't see Josie that day atall an' it was well after dinner time the nixt day before a was able te sit up an' take notice. Be that time Josie was up an' walkin' about as right as rain even though she didn't feel much like talkin'. If Josie wasn't in a mood for talkin' that wasn't the problem way the oul wan in the other bed. She niver let up from when she woke in the mornin' till she went te sleep at night.

After our operations me an' Josie foun' it harder te listen te hir because we weren't feelin' too hot oursel's. Te make matters worse didn't Doctor Ali, the black doctor that the oul wan hated, take a great shine te me. Ivery time he got aff duty he come an' set down beside me bed te houl me han' an' chat te me. He wouldn't call me Ann atall but said me name was Fatima. He niver left the ward at night till a had gone te sleep. That only made the oul wan worse so she took a wile bad turn agen me allthegether because the name that he called me reminded hir of a place in Portugal where effin popish scum claimed that the mother of god cured all their disease.

Wan evenin' when me an' Josie had been in hospital for nearly a week we were at our wits en' tryin' te think of a way te shut the oul doll up. Josie said that it might be the aisiest thing in the worl' te put a pilla over hir face an' sit on it for a wheen of minutes but a allowed that it would cause more trouble than it was worth because the two of us would just get hung.

Then a had a better idea. When nobody on our ward was too ill, all the nurses went aff at eight a-clock ivery night te have their tay. If we wanted te call wan of them we had te press a button that rung a bell down in the canteen. That night, as soon as the coast was clear, the two of us jumped outa bed, put on our slippers an' dressin' gowns an' went over te the oul wan in the bed in the corner. Josie stood between hir an' the button so as she couldn't call for help when a was windin' the wheels of hir bed down. Then a pushed hir, bed an' all, outa the ward an' down a long corridor te the back of the hospital where the mortuary was. Josie stood guard.

As luck would have it the place was as silent as the grave so a just went in an' set hir bed up beside a corpse that was covered in a sheet. She got wile subdued then an' started te plead way me not te lave hir there but a toul hir that she was just te make hirsel' at home an' continue on the way she always was an' hir oul screechin' might do some good for a change an' waken the dead. Then a went out an' closed the door an' me an' Josie run back to our beds.

When Doctor Ali come te visit me that night the first thing he noticed was the absence of abuse the minute he walked in the door. He asked me where the oul doll was so a just said, the poor creathure, she died. That's impossible, he said, a'm the only doctor on duty an' a would have had te confirm hir death. Then a said, o a'm sorry, but a didn't know that or a would have sent for ye. When she died, a just took hir down an' put hir in the mortuary, poor soul.

Doctor Ali jumped up an' run down the corridor an' burst inte the mortuary an' that oul wan was niver as glad te see a human face in the whole of hir life even though the colour of it didn't suit hir very much. The nurses were all very cross in a light wee way way me an' Josie an' when they took the oul wan outa the mortuary they put hir inte a different ward so we niver seen hir again. When Doctor Ali come back te see me he sat down beside me bed way a wile serious look on hes face an' he wagged hes finger at me an' said, o naughty, naughty Fatima.

A got outa the hospital an' went on the sick an' the money was great. Twice as much as a got for workin' forty-six hours in the factory. A was lucky too because our doctor thought that a wasn't big or strong enough te be workin' atall so ivery time a went te see him he asked me how a was feelin' an' when he heard that a was gran' he just wrote me out another sick note an' toul me te see him in a month.

It begin te occur te me that a could make good use outa me new-foun' wealth — four poun' ten shillin's a week. Te start way a decided te get a maid for me ma so as she wouldn't have te do any more hard work. When the maid was doin' all the work in our house a planned te get mesel' an education be goin' te the library in our town an' readin' ivery book in it.

All the rich weemen in our town kept maids an' paid them two poun's a week. They had te start work at seven a-clock in the mornin' an' finish at seven a-clock at night way ivery third Sunday afternoon aff. A decided te give our maid three poun' an' let hir work any hours that suited hir.

It didn't take me long te get a woman te do the work for me ma because the first wan a asked jumped at the idea. A had trouble gettin' hir te wait till the nixt day for she said there was nothin' stappin' hir startin' right away. She had worked as a maid aff an' on for years te different people in our town an' was wile well known as a great wee worker. She was the same wee woman that had passed by our school on the day me da got outa jail.

The first day that she landed at our house a nearly drapped down dead because she didn't call me Ann as she had always done before but Miss McGlone instead. A took hir upstairs in a hurry te explain te hir that she should call me Ann because a just hated te be called Miss McGlone. She said it was only right an' proper te call the young mistress Miss like she had been taught. A toul hir that a was no young mistress atall an' she was te think of me as if a was her daughter or hir niece or somebody like that. Then she took out hir hankie an' blew hir nose an' said that niver in hir life before did she work for such dasent people.

A went down stairs te make some tay for hir an' me ma who was lyin' in hir bed in the back room dyin' from the menopause. A poured out the tay an' called the wee woman down for a sup, then a realised she was takin' on far more work than was needed. She appeared at the kitchen door heavin' a big mattress behine hir. She just wouldn't listen te me pleadin' not te stress hirsel' but took all the mattresses from upstairs out inte the back yard te beat them an' give them an airin' before she made the beds.

A didn't like te see hir doin' all that hard work on hir own so when a couldn't manage te stap hir a had te set te helpin' hir instead. When the two of us were out in the back yard beatin' the mattresses the two neighbours on either side come out te laugh an' pass remarks because the wee woman was a protestant. As we heaved the mattresses back inte the house a tried te explain te hir again that a didn't want hir killin' hersel' workin'.

She said that she wasn't killin' hersel' atall an' that this was the aisiest job she iver done in hir life because there wasn't always somebody lookin' over hir shoulder tellin' hir what te do. Then a realised that a was as bad mesel', standin' over the poor soul tellin' hir what not te do so a went away an' left hir in pase.

She cleaned the whole upstairs an' scrubbed the floors that first day an' a was glad when she was finished because a felt wile guilty seein' hir workin' like that an' hir even ouler than me ma.

As soon as she left our house that day, me ma got outa hir bed an' started te examine all the work that had been done. After careful scrutiny me ma concluded that the wee woman done a sloppy job. A toul hir that if a worked in the factory she would have te do all the work hirsel' so she shouldn't be too eager te criticise people who were tryin' te make hir life aisier for hir. Me ma said that there was nobody doin' hir no favours an' that the woman was gettin' paid for it. A toul me ma that she was a bitch.

Me ma started te scream an' faint an' tell me that she was over forty years oul an' that niver in hir life had she called hir mother a bitch. A said te me ma that that was maybe because hir mother niver deserved it. Me ma flew at me an' tried te murder me an' said what little thanks she got for rearin' a wan like me. A toul me ma that she had niver reared me because a had reared mesel' an' all hir other wains as well. After that me ma went te hir bed pantin' an' a started te think that maybe she wasn't all that different from the oul wan that had been in hospital way me an' Josie.

That night a went along te the house of the wee woman te tell hir that she could have the nixt day aff. She got inte a terrible state an' started te question me about whether a had foun' hir work good enough. A

69

toul hir that it was so good that she had done two days work in wan.

A spent all the nixt day tryin' te make up te me ma for the words a had had way hir but she only stapped huffin' long enough te list te me all the things she had iver done for me in the whole of me life as if a was likely te forget them anyway.

The nixt day, the wee woman landed in early because she couldn't wait te get on way hir job. The minute she came in she didn't even bother te stap for the sup of tay that a wanted te make hir but rushed straight up the stairs an' opened all the windows an' made beds an' dusted an' cleaned till a was fair ashamed of mesel' for readin' books.

When she come downstairs she lifted all the mats an' took them outside an' hung them on the clothesline. She come back in an' started on the scullery an' what a bit of cleanin' she didn't do te it (an' it wasn't its neighbours that needed it). Ivery shelf an' cupboard, ivery nook an' cranny got turned inside out. It took hir most of the day te get the house inte the kine of shape she wanted it an' a stayed well outa me ma's way in case she foun' anythin' te complain' about.

When it was comin' up te five a-clock a tried te get the wee woman te lave before me da would land home from hes work but a couldn't do a damn thing te shift hir. There she was makin' me da's dinner in the nice spick-an'-span scullery, an' boilin' water up on the range for hes wash. A toul hir that me da washed himsel' in coul water, twice a day, three hundred an' sixty five days a year, an' that he'd always done that iver since he was a wee wain, but it did no good. A just knew that if some miracle didn't happen te get hir te go home before me da arrived a might say goodbye te me ma's maid.

In our house there was a drawer where me ma kept good things for an emergency, sheets, an' a clean towel, in case the doctor had te be called in a hurry, an' a gran' tablecloth made outa Irish linen te be put on the table if it happened te be clear when she spotted a priest comin' headin' in the gate.

While the wee woman was cleanin' out the drawers she spotted these things an' low-an'-behold what did she do but take the gran' Irish linen cloth out an' spread it on the table for me da's dinner. A said a prayer te St Jude that me da would have overtime that night or that hes Norton 250 would break down or that the groun' would just open up an' swalley the whole bloody lot of us, but as was usual way all my prayers, nobody was listenin' te them.

He's a very predictable sort of a man, me da. The neighbours actually set their clocks by him. When he comes inte the scullery at five a-clock on the dot ivery day he closes the door behine him an' takes hes milk bottle an' lunch box outa hes bag. Then he hangs hes bag up on a nail on the back door an' comes over an' closes the door between the kitchen an' the scullery. Then he has hes wash an' changes inte hes clean clothes that are left hangin' on a nail on the back of the scullery door. Then he hangs hes workin' clothes up on the same nail an' opens the scullery door an' comes inte the kitchen an' kisses me ma an' says te hir, anythin' strange the day, Maggie? at exactly a quarter past five. Then he sits down at the tap of the table an' ates hes dinner an' says te me ma, that was nice, Maggie.

Well, that day things were very different, not that me da didn't land in the back door at five a-clock on the dot, for he did. But the minute he closed the door behind him iverythin' changed. The wee woman come rushin' out an' took the lunch box from hes han' an' started emptin' it hirsel'. She then run inte the kitchen an' come tearin' out way a big pipin' hot tub of water an' presented me da way the good towel that me ma had put away for emergencies.

71

A made sure te avoid me da's eyes for a knew that he was rippin' mad way me, for not only did he hate hot water an' fussin' weemen but the worst thing in the worl' happened. The wee woman who had known me da on first name terms for well over thirty years, took te callin' him Sir. When this happened a had a heavy heart because a knew that a was goin' te have te say goodbye te me ma's maid foriver. That was the last attempt a made to make me ma's life aisey for many a long day.

After a was on the sick for six months an' gettin' well used te it, a letter landed for me wan day, tellin' me that a was te attend a medical board te be examined. The medical board said that a was in perfect health so a wasn't able te stay on the sick any longer. Then me ma an' da said that they couldn't afford to keep me so a would have te go back te the factory again.

A toul me ma an' da that they had no need te keep me for a had decided te lave home. They said, ye'll do no such thing, me lady, ye'r too young te be lavin' home, ye'll stay in this house way us till the day an' hour ye get married. A allowed that at that rate of goin' a would be at home for a quare long time because a had no intention of iver gettin' married.

If me ma had of went te any hops hirsel' an' seen the kine of boys that were at them she mightn't have been so keen on talkin' about me marryin'. They were no Beatles them, oh no, they didn't want te hold yer hand or love ye, yeah, yeah, yeah. All they wanted te do was ate big pieces outa the side of yer neck or shove their slevery oul tongues down yer throat till ye were damn near choked, or grope aroun' way their dirty hacked oul han's inside yer knickers when they had ye pasted to the nearest wall without even askin' ye yer name.

A could see that me ma an' da had their plans laid, for me te carry on workin' in the factory till a married wan of these boyos, an' a wanted none of it. A decided then an' there that a might as well do some good in the worl' instead, but a must of been headin' in the wrong direction, for a ended up in a convent.

Wheniver a toul me ma an' da that a wanted te be a nun, me da tried to get me te change me mine be gowling' an' shoutin' an' sayin' that a would go away te be a bloody nun over hes dead body, me lady. A toul me da that a thought it a cryin' shame that he planned to die so young an' lave me poor ma a lonely widda woman. When a said that me da took a swipe at me an' missed for he wasn't a very good shot.

He kept on gowlin' at me ivery day till the very day the nuns landed at our house te interview me. Then me da got feared that a was maybe goin' te go away after all an' that he would niver see me again so he started te be wile nice te me allthegether instead.

A wheen of weeks before a was due te go inte the convent, a took a wile yearnin' for life an' got it inte me head that if a didn't get te see Brendan Boyer doin' the Hucklebuck just wan time before a went away a would probably die. When a made this announcement te me family they were highly delighted.

The Royal Showband was makin' a tour of the north of Ireland at the time, an' weren't they comin' te our town just two nights before a was due te go away. Me ma an' da took this as a blessin' in disguise an' a fair enough indication of how the lord could be seen te act in strange an' mysterious ways. Me da put himsel' inte debt be buyin' me a gran' new frock, me big brother bought me a pair of red shoes way heels on them seven inches high, an' me ma surpassed hirsel' completely be getting' me lipstick an' powder te put on me face, a thing she'd forbid me te do in the past.

On the night of the dance when a landed at the hall way me big brother, there were two thousand other people standin' waitin' te get in an' we were nearly kilt in the crush as soon as the doors opened. In the first

73

half of the night, some wee band from the back of beyond come on te play for us, but the two thousand people threw pennies at them an' shouted at them te get aff. (In them days pennies were fairly big things.)

Be the time Brendan Boyer an' the Royal Showband got up on the stage te play, a had managed te fight me way forward te the front of the hall an' get mesel' inte a quare good position te view the Hucklebuck. It was ivery thing a had iver imagined it te be an' a was so delighted that be the time the dance was over a had plucked up courage te go an' ask Brendan Boyer for hes autograph. A toul him that a was goin' away te a convent an' a would niver see him again so he wrote hes name on me arm an' asked me to pray for him. A toul him a would, ivery day, an' a would niver wash me arm again for the rest of me life. Well, a prayed for him ivery day all right but a had to wash me arm a lot sooner than a thought.

Wheniver a got home that night a was ten feet seven inches aff the groun' an' me ma an' da were waitin' up te hear how a had got on. A toul them all about the dance an' showed them the autograph an' me da said a could look forward te a lot of other gran' nights like that wan an' forget all this oul nun business an' enjoy mesel' when a was young. Me ma said that me da was right, an' if a still wanted te be a nun when a was twenty, hir an' me da would be only too willin' te encourage me.

If a could of thought of some fool-proof way of keepin' things as they were at that very minute a would gladly have called the whole thing aff, but a knew that me da was playin' hes trump card an' as soon as a'd respond the only thing he'd have te offer was sendin' me back te the factory so a said te him, da, a'm goin'.

The day a landed at the convent, the first thing the nuns done was sen' me aff way another young girl te get dressed up in the garments. While we were walkin' up the corridor a spoke te hir, just to be civil an' pass the time of day. She niver answered me but she put hir han' te hir lips an' looked real startled. A could of kicked mesel' for openin' me mouth an' a wondered at the unkindness of the other nuns for not warnin' me that the poor girl was mute. A got the shock of me life a wheen of moments later when we got te the tap of the stairs, for didn't she pull me sleeve an' beckon me te folly hir inte a doorway so she could confab way me. It was then a discovered that nuns weren't allowed te talk but it didn't bother me much because a had niver been wile fond of talkin' te nuns anyway.

Wheniver a come down dressed up in the garments me ma burst inte tears at the sight of me because a looked like somethin' no woman could iver have given birth te. Me da was about te give me a big hug but he thought the better of it when he seen the face of the oul Reverent Mother tellin' him that a would have te go te the chapel so he just shook han's way me instead. A took a wile big deep breath an' said nothin' an' made sure not te look at me ma an' da in case they would know what a was thinkin'.

After they went away a was glad that the nuns had this rule of silence because a knew that me voice wouldn't be workin' right. When we come outa the chapel after prayin' for a wheen of hours, we had our supper, a gran' big feed. While we were aten, wan of the young nuns was readin' out loud te us all about how poor St Maria Goretti got hirsel' raped an' brutally murdered an' a allowed that if anythin' in this worl' could be worse than me grannie's banquets, then this was it.

After supper the nuns brought me upstairs where they had a big do arranged te welcome me an' another girl called Una, from Athlone in County Westmeath. Una was twenty-one an' it turned out that she had an identical twin sister who went aff an' left hir te marry some man. The other young nuns sung songs, an' played music, an' recited poems, an' danced for the two of us an' a was delighted till the Reverent Mother turned roun' an' toul me that it was my turn. A thought she was makin' a joke on account of the fact that most people a had met before that time had had a sense of humour so a laughed it aff accordingly.

That was the first mistake a made in the convent. No, it wasn't really, come te think, it was just the first mistake a was aware of at the time. Later on a learned that nuns weren't allowed te cross their legs because it wasn't ladylike.

The nixt mornin' after mass, the mother of novices took me inte hir office an' toul me te kneel on the floor, so a did. Then she started te list aff all the rules of the convent te me. The first wan was custody of the eyes. That meant that a was te learn te be shifty an' niver te look at a body if a was tallkin' te them but te look at the floor instead. Then she toul me the rule a knew about anyway only she called it custody of the lips. That meant that a was not only te be shifty but a was te walk right by people without even botherin' te pass them the time of day.

When she toul me a was always te keep custody of the han's an' niver te touch another nun a allowed that that wouldn't bother me much. The nixt rule was the worst rule of them all. She toul me that a would have te tittle-tattle te the Reverent Mother or hir if a iver seen wan of the other nuns breakin' the rules. A allowed there an' then that a would need te take great pains niver te see what any of the other nuns were doin' but that if perchance a slipped up, a would just have te make do way an oul rule of me ma's — niver go stickin' yer nose inte other people's business.

That mornin' when a'd been at mass a took me period, so as soon as a could get a word in edgeways a asked hir could a have some sanitary towels. She set aff an' landed back a wheen of minutes later way a pile of blood-stained cloths an' handed them te me. A toul hir that a didn't want them because somebody else had been usin' them. Well, she didn't take that very well atall an' she launched inte me way a new lecture as long as the day an' the morrow, about learnin' obedience an' humility an' how self-will hinders the search for perfection an' holiness an' how a must learn te turn away from all earthly desires an' give mesel' over completely te god. She said that a must always bear in mine how great an' manifole were the gifts that god bestowed on them that loved him.

A allowed that at that rate of goin' these nuns musta loved god a quare good bit because it appeared te me that the seven poun' that a had brought them for sanitary protection was a great an' manifole gift indeed considerin' what they were sellin'. As if that wasn't bad enough, she then took a whip way leather thongs that had wee bits of lead fastened te the en's of them outa hir drawer an' showed it te me an' toul me that it was called the discipline. She demonstrated how it worked be beatin' hersel' on the back way it.

Before ye go away te be a nun ye have te go te a doctor te have yer head examined te see if ye'r mental, an' if ye happen te be foun' te be mental, the nuns will have nothin' atall te do way ye. Now it was just as well that a'd had me head looked at before a went inte the convent because if a hadn't have, a would of been askin' mesel' questions about me own sanity, for here was this woman standin' in front of me, flayin' hirsel' way a whip, an' me kneelin' there watchin' hir doin' it way the blood runnin' down me thighs.

Wheniver she was finished flayin' hirsel' she handed the whip te me an' said that it was no longer obligatory te use it but that if a had a fervent desire te strive after holiness a might fine it useful an' a could keep it in the locker beside me bed an' beat mesel' way it ivery night before a went te sleep. She warned me te be careful not te make any marks on mesel' way it before the followin' Wednesday when a doctor was comin' te give Una an' me a thorough physical examination (te see if we were pregnant a suppose).

Well, seein' as it wasn't compulsary te whip mesel', a decided te decline hir kind offer of the whip so a said te hir that a would try te strive after holiness some other way. That didn't please hir very much so she launched inte me way a new lecture an' at the en' of it she give me penance te do in the middle of the refectory when all the other nuns were aten up their supper.

On the followin' Wednesday, Una an' me had te stay in our beds till after the doctor examined us. He examined me first because my bed was nearest te the door, an' low-an'behold didn't he spot the autograph on me arm an' ask me all about it. A toul him how a had been te see the Hucklebuck an' he toul me that hes daughter was a great Brendan Boyer fan an' that even hes wife liked him an' thought that hes voice compared in quality an' range te that of Elvis Presley, an' a agreed.

As soon as the doctor left the dormitory, the mother of novices who had been present at the examination, ordered me te get dressed at once an' go te the Reverent Mother's office. Wheniver a got there, the dressin' down the two of them give me surpassed any dressin' down a had iver had before. They said a was defilin' the holy cloister be houlin' on te worldy desires, an' when a went up the stairs te wash the autograph aff me arm a felt like the greatest sinner iver born even though a knew a shouldn't because a had niver kilt anybody.

Before a was in the convent very long a foun' out that a wasn't te be allowed te do any good in the worl' atall because a would have te spen' the rest of me life gettin' detached an' savin' me soul be imitatin' Christ. Accordin' te this book that was wrote be a Thomas A. Kempis, if ye didn't turn yer back on iverybody in the worl', ye didn't stan' a snowball's chance in hell of iver gettin' inte heaven.

It saddened me somethin' shockin' allthegether when a thought of the fate that lay before me poor ma an' da because they weren't imitatin' Christ, for there was no way that a body could iver imitate Christ an' manage te live in our house at the same time. A knew a was supposed te be detached, but someway a could niver get detached enough te think of livin' happy up in heaven for iver an' iver while me poor ma an' da were burnin' down in hell.

A thought hard of a way te get me da te take te the drink an' learn te walk on water an' a concluded that it might just be possible, but wheniver a reflected on the total futility of tryin' te turn me poor ma back inte a virgin again a give up in despair. But a'm not a wan that despairs for very long about anythin' so a soon started te look for ways outa me dilemma.

The first thing a done then was read Thomas A. Kempis's book a couple more times te see if a could fine any loopholes in it an' a did. Te begin way, for a body that done so much preachin' about humility, he didn't seem te have a lot of it himsel' for he was foriver talkin' on about what god thought about iverythin' like he was privy te the mine of god, or was even god himsel'. A don't know why the superiors were always goin' on about how great he was because if a body reads hes book anyway well atall the only reasonable conclusion they could possibly come te was that the man was a terrible oul fanatic an' cod allthegether, that couldn't put two consecutive words on a page without contradictin' himsel'.

The hardest thing about life in the convent was the lack of human contact. The voice of god was the only thing that we were allowed te hear, an' the voice of god had no human warmth. It was the cold metallic peal of a bell, tellin' us when te rise, when te pray, when te ate, when te study, when te work an' when te go back te bed again. A often wondered what the other nuns thought about it but a wasn't able te ask them. A niver thought very highly of it mesel' though. For me it could niver compensate atall for the gentle caress of me da's voice sayin' te me at twelve a-clock at night, gone te yer bed ye bastard ye or a'll fell ye.

It would have been intolerably borin' in the convent a suppose if it hadn't been for the fact that we were took out for two wee trips ivery year. In May we went te visit a shrine in Knock where Our Lady appeared te the Irish in the nineteenth century an' said nothin' te them atall, on account of the fact that anythin' she might of felt like sayin' would have been exaggerated outa all proportion an' be the en' of six months would have meant somethin' quite different from what she had intended, so she just looked at them instead.

The other annual excursion we made was te a place called Glendalough, in the County of Wicklow, te visit the tomb of wan of Ireland's most revered sons, the Holy Saint Kevin, patron saint of woman-beaters.

Wheniver a was in the convent for six months the nuns toul me that a was te get married te Christ an' that a bishop was te perform the ceremony. The night before the weddin' a had curlin' pins put in me hair an' on the mornin' of the big day all the other nuns started te fuss over me. They dressed me up in a weddin' frock an' put a wreath an' a veil on me head. They got me te stan' way me han's joined thegether an' a wile holy lookin' face on me te have me weddin' photo took.

Una was gettin' married te Christ the same day as me an' a lot of other nuns were makin' vows of wan kine or another so we had te go in a procession te the altar. A had te go up the aisle first because a was the baby nun on account of the fact that a was the youngest girl in the convent. When a got up te the altar the bishop was standin' there waitin' an' he said te me, what is it that ye seek child, in the latin tongue, so a said te him, *mihi absit gloriari, nisi in cruce domini nostri Jesi Christi, per quem mihi mundus crucifixus est et ego mundo,* an' he musta been pleased enough way me answer for he picked up a pair of scissors an' started te cut the hair aff me.

As soon as he had finished hes job of barberin', two nuns come up behine me an' took me weddin' frock aff. Then the bishop put the holy habit on me while the two of us confabbed away in latin. After he was finished marryin' me to Christ, the bishop toul me that a was no longer te be called Ann an' he give me a new name, a real holy-soundin' name that a had niver heard before in all me life. Then he give me a lit candle an' said te me, go show yer light te the worl'.

Because of the importance of the occasion, the nuns wrote a letter te me ma an' da askin' them te be present te see their daughter gettin' married. Wheniver a was leadin' the procession up the aisle a kept proper custody of the eyes as befitted me status as a bride of Christ but nivertheless a couldn't help noticin' that me ma an' da weren't in the chapel. A took te worryin' then that maybe they'd had an accident an' gone over the ditch somewhere in the oul crock of a car that me da was sure te have borrowed for the day. Well, when a turned roun' te show me light te the worl' for the very first time what did a see but me ma an' da sittin' up in the front of the chapel in the seats that had been reserved for them.

A had been practisin' religious decorum ivery day for six months an' a was fairly good at lookin' holy be this time but me face went away an' let me down the very minute a turned roun' be breakin' out of its own accord inte a big beam of a relieved smile at the sight of me ma an' da safe that toul the Reverent Mother that a was still houlin' on tight te worldly concerns.

After all the ceremony was over a went te the refectory way the other nuns te have the weddin' feast. It was the greatest feed a had iver seen in me life but a didn't know what wan half of the things a was aten were on account of the fact that a wasn't allowed to ask.

A went te the parlour after that te meet me ma an' da an' a was so delighted te see them that a nearly jumped on the two of them the way a had jumped on me da the day me wee sister was born but a didn't for fear the Reverent Mother would give me more penance te do because a was fed up te the teeth way penance already.

Me ma an' da brought me wee sister an' two of me wee brothers way them. Me big brother was invited too but he refused te come, sayin' that if a wanted te bury mesel' alive there was nothin' he could do te stap me but he was damned if he was goin' te look at me doin' it. Me wee sister an' brothers made a quare bad impression on the Reverent Mother. She asked me wee sister if she wanted te be a nun like me an' me wee sister said te hir, naw. Then she said te me wee sister, why do you not want to be a nun, child? an' me wee sister said te hir, because a want te be a wife like me ma.

Me two wee brothers would do nothin' atall but fight an' wrestle on the convent lawn that people weren't even allowed te walk on so me ma had te keep on tryin' te stap them in case they would ruin their good suits. The two of them didn't talk te me atall because they thought a was a nun but they looked at me suspiciously when they thought a didn't notice because of the custody of the eyes that a appeared te be keepin'.

Wheniver the Reverent Mother's back was turned me ma said te me, Ann, a mean sister, ye'v got bigger. A said te me ma, ma, don't call me sister, me name is Ann. Me ma said, god forgiv' ye for showin' such disrespect, of course yer name is sister now, an' a allowed that me ma's menopause musta come back te have another go at hir. Then me ma started te tell me about the great feed of sandwiches that the nuns had give hir an' me da an' the wains. She asked me was a gettin' enough te ate in the convent an' a toul hir that the food was great allthegether but she wouldn't believe me because of the vow of poverty. She nearly drapped down dead wheniver a toul hir about the two glasses of wine a had had way the weddin' feast because she had got me te take the pledge when a was fourteen, niver te touch alcoholic drink in the whole of me life. A had te explain te me ma that things like pledges were nothin' more than worldly concerns an' could have no place in the life of a religious.

Before me ma an' da went away that night me ma took a big wad of notes outa hir han'bag an' toul me that it was money the people of our town had give te me da an' hir te bring te me. A could hardly believe me eyes an' a said te me ma that it was wile big of the people of our town te mine about me after a had been gone such a long time. A said that seein' as the money was mine a would like te see it used te buy me ma a washin' machine. She wouldn't hear of the like an' said that a must give it te the missions. A toul me ma that she WAS the missions an' a tried te pull rank on hir be pointin' out that a was a nun an' knew more about the missions than she done but that didn't work on me ma.

When a tried te give the money te me da he looked aroun' te see if any of the other nuns were lookin' an' they weren't so he give me a big hug an' said, that's my Ann, but he wouldn't take the money either. After that a tried te get me wee brothers an' sister te take it but they just shied away from me way their han's in their pockets. In the en' a had te give all that money te the oul Reverent Mother an' she had no objection te pocketin' it.

Four months after that day the mistress of novices toul me that a was te go te the city te help the directoress of vocations te do some shoppin'. A was scared stiff when a heard it because a hadn't been out shoppin' for such a long time but a done what a was toul an' went away in the big car way blacked out windows. As soon as we arrived at the shoppin' part of the city, the directoress, who was drivin' the car, toul me te go te the post office an' buy wan an' eleven pence worth of stamps. She put hir han' inte the slit at the side of hir habit an' took out half-a-crown an' handed it te me. A looked at it way wonder because a had forgot what a half-crown looked like.

A asked the directoress if she was comin' too but she said she would stay in the car. It had been ten months since a'd been out on a busy street so a walked along feelin' kinda strange, keepin' custody of the eyes as best a could in the way the nuns had taught me. A was about te go inte the post office when this wee wain of about four year oul come chargin' roun' a corner an' bumped straight inte me. A was all delighted because a hadn't seen such a wee wain in months. A crouched down on me hunkers an' said te it, hello wain, what's your name? an' a patted it on the head. The wee wain was lookin' at me wonderin' what kine of a rare creature a was when its ma landed on the scene pushin' a pram an' draggin' another wain of about two year oul be the han'.

She started te apologise for hir wain bumpin' inte me an' a said that it was all right. Then she spotted me accent an' said te me, de ye come from the north? an' a said a did. The two of us went on te confab about wains an' things an' soon a whole crowd of people had gathered roun' te look at me. There was a wile lot of pushin' an' jundyin' goin' on an' some oul wan started shoutin' at all the people goin' by on the street te for god's sake come quick an' have a look at this lovely wee nun. Before long, people were takin' out their purses an' tryin' te give me money te pray for them an' a was standin' there not knowin' what te do so in the en' a started te pray te St Jude again that the groun' would open up an' swally me, but it didn't.

Wheniver a got back te the convent a was sent straight away te the Reverent Mother's office where a foun' out that the directoress didn't take me out te help way the shoppin' atall. She only brought me out te watch for any signs of worldliness in me an' it seems that she spotted plenty.

Chapter 5

A would have stayed in the convent till a grew outa it, which mighta took a long time (my family are not famous for growin') if the Reverent Mother hadn't been watchin' me carefully all the time. Wan day she discovered that a was possessed be the divil. As soon as she foun' out about me affliction the Reverent Mother wrote a lyin' letter te me ma an' da tellin' them that a wanted te lave the convent an' askin' them te come an' pick me up on a certin date.

Me da wrote back te me straight away tellin' me that he would come for me on the very day that a got hes letter an' all a needed te do was phone him te confirm that a was ready at a number he give me three different times just te make sure a got it right. A would have phoned me da up right enough if a hada got the letter that he sent me but the oul Reverent Mother kept it for hirself an' answered me da on my behalf, tellin' him that the date she mentioned before would be most suitable, so me da took a week aff hes work te sit beside a telephone for nothin'.

The first time a knew a was goin' home was when the mother of novices' assistant come up to me wan day when we were in the choir practisin' the hymn, 'Ye

Can Tell We Are Christians By Our Love, By Our Love, Ye Can Tell We Are Christians By Our Love', an' said te me, go te the superior's office.

When me an' hir landed at the superior's office she looked surprised te fine that nobody was there but she kept proper custody of all hir senses as best she could under the circumstances till the telephone rang te relieve hir. She lifted up the receiver in fear an' trepidation an' listened, without keepin' proper custody of her ears, because she appeared te hear what was bein' said on the other side.

After she was finished on the telephone, the mother of novices' assistant said, follow me, an' a said te mesel', now where did a hear that before? A walked after hir till a came te a part of the convent a had niver been in before an' she sent me inte a strange wee room. The Reverent Mother was there. The only bit of furniture in the room was a table an' my suitcase was sittin' on it. The Reverent Mother said te me, take off your habit an' dress in yer secular clothes, then leave by that door, your father is waitin' in the car park. Wheniver a was finished changin', the Reverent Mother said, goodbye sister, an' used the real holy-soundin' name that the bishop had give me on the day he had cut me hair. A looked at hir an' said, there's no need te call me that now Reverent Mother, my name is Ann Elizabeth McGlone.

A got out the door an' me da seen me comin' an' run te meet me. He couldn't believe hes eyes seein' me way me nuns' hair cut in me oul clothes that didn't fit anymore, so he took aff hes own big long overcoat an' wrapped me up in it. As we were drivin' up the road me da said te me, for god's sake, why couldn't ye have rung me up like a asked ye te in the letter, a could have brought ye some new clothes te wear if a had been toul ye needed them.

A said te me da, what letter did ye write me? an' he said he had wrote to me seven times in the past month since the Reverent Mother's letter arrived te announce that a wanted te come home. A toul me da that a had got none of hes letters an' the first time a knew a was goin' home was ten minutes before a met him in the car park.

Me da then stapped the car an' started te quiz me. Then he turned the car roun' an' headed back in the direction of the convent way a wile murderous look on hes face. A started to cry wheniver a thought of me da havin' to go te jail for the rest of his life for killin' a Reverent Mother, an' also at the thought of havin' te look at the god-damned convent again. Ma da stapped the car te try te get me te quit cryin' but a wouldn't till he turned the car back in the direction of home.

On our way home me da was in a quare oul state allthegether, tryin' te think of a way te get me a feed without lettin' people see the cut of me. He left me sittin' in the car two or three times, te go searchin' for a cafe, before he foun' wan that suited him. Then he come an' took me outa the car, still wrapped up in hes big coat, an' the two of us went in the back door of a cafe an' landed in a kitchen way a big turf fire. An oul woman set the two of us down te a big feed an' said what a quare load of oul villains all nuns were.

We got home late at night an' wile tired an me ma couldn't have seemed less delighted te see me if she hada tried. Wheniver a seen the look on hir face me stomach started te do somersaults of its own free will because it could see for itsel' that a wasn't wanted. Durin' the time a was in the convent me ma was delighted way hirsel' for bein' lucky enough te have a daughter a nun. She was foriver tellin' hir frien's about how a was born te be a nun, an' how well suited te the convent a was, an' how a had now a gran' holy-soundin' name, an' how a looked for all the worl' like wan of them wee holy pictures that a body keeps in their prayer book, an' how they wouldn't know me from Adam if perchance they spotted me in the gran' swanky nuns' uniform. So that was the reason why me ma wasn't delighted te see me when a landed home lookin' like a scarecrow that was badly put thegether in a wile hell of a hurry an' nothin' te be writin' home about atall.

Wheniver a was in the convent, the nuns give me elocution lessons that spoilt me whole natural way of talkin' for many a long day afterwards. As soon as a spoke a word te me ma she said back te me, a don't know where you intend te sleep the night but a'm sure this house won't be gran' enough for a lady like you way such a posh way of puttin' on airs an' graces. A tried te give me ma a hug but she pushed me away an' said, get outa me sight will ye, so a started to cry. Me da then started shoutin' at me ma te have a bit of bloody wit woman, for couldn't she see for hirsel' that the poor wain had suffered enough, but me ma didn't believe that anybody in the worl' was capable of sufferin' but hirsel', so she carried on insultin' me till she was tired an' ready te go te hir bed.

Me da toul me that a would be better te go te me own bed too, so a went up the stairs inte the room that a had shared way me five wee sisters before a went away, an' a foun' me own place in the bed beside me wee sister that me da said he got especially for me because a had too many brothers.

The nixt mornin', instead of the sound of the convent bell, a heard me ma's voice screamin' at the bottom of the stairs for all the dirty rotten good-for-nothin' blaggards of the day that were lying stinkin' in their beds, te get up before she made them sorry that they didn't heed hir warnin'.

A got up right away an' come down the stairs. It was half-past six so a decided te go for a walk as a could think of nothin' else to do. A toul me ma that a would go out te give hir a chance te get the wains up, an' then she started screamin' at me about puttin' on airs an' graces again, an' who did a think a was? A said te hir that a didn't think a was anybody. Me ma grabbed me be the hair an' started to shake me an' say, a nice fool ye managed te make outa all of us, me lady. How de ye think a'm iver goin' te be able te houl me head up in this town again, after all them people givin' me all that money for you, an' me takin' it from them thinkin' ye were goin' te make yer mother proud? Now ye think ye can just land back in here, puttin' on airs an' graces like the rest of us weren't good enough for ye. A said nothin' an' just looked at me ma an' after she let me hair go a went out inte the scullery an' started to wash the dishes.

As soon as the wains went out te school that day, weemen started te come te our house te get lookin' at me an' te ask me what it was like te live in a convent. Some of the weemen were the mothers of nuns who were worried about their daughters an' they asked me were the Reverent Mothers cruel an' did a think that anybody could ever be happy in a convent an' did the nuns get enough te ate an' were they warm enough in their beds at night or did they really sleep in coffins an' whip themsel's an' wear chains way nails stickin' inte their flesh?

Some of the other weemen wanted to know what kine of knickers ye wear in a convent, an' did ye stap havin' periods wance ye were there, an' did ye keep on all yer clothes te have a bath, an' was it true that all the pubic hair on the body fell aff an' the breasts shrunk the minute the holy habit was put on? A set there watchin' them an' listenin' te what they were sayin' an' a come te the conclusion that there wasn't a hope in hell of me iver gettin' through te St Jude because he was bound te be booked-up solid for all eternity dealin' way all the other hopeless cases in the worl' so he could have no time for me.

Wheniver the word landed in our town that a was te be comin' home from the convent, some weemen that kept maids allowed that a would be a great kine of a skivvy te have aroun' their houses te break the monotony of their lives be answerin' all their questions about convents. Before a even knew that a was comin' home, three of these weemen come te our house an' toul me ma that she had no need te worry about me gettin' a dasent job because they would be only too delighted te give me a start.

In the middle of me first mornin' home me ma toul me that a would be better te make up me mine quick which of these weemen a wanted te work for an' get outa hir sight before she done somethin' she might regret. A went te wan that had only recently moved te our town an' who had two wains an' was expectin' hir third in a wheen of weeks because a liked wee wains an' a reckoned that the divil ye didn't know couldn't be any worse than the divil ye did, but he might, way a wee bit of luck, be better.

Well, this woman had a gran' house, an' two beautiful wains, an' six wardrobes full of clothes, an' two real fur coats, an' seventy-nine pairs of shoes not countin' boots an' slippers, an' hundreds of kines of make-up an' perfume, an' a car of hir own, an' a husband that worked nearly twenty-four hours a day, an' no frien's.

She didn't really want me te do any work. All she really asked from me was that a sit listenin' te hir talk, an' call hir be hir first name wheniver there was nobody else about, an' admire all hir frocks, an' tell hir what a thought of all the girls she used te work way for bein' jealous of hir for havin' married such a good goer, an' criticise all the big bugs in our town for cockin' their snooks at hir because she had only worked in a shop before she was married, an' tell hir that she was just as good as them an' knew how te treat hir maid like an ordinary human bein' not like them, an' sit up way hir till the middle of the night when hir husband come home an' drove me back te our house.

A thought me ma would be pleased way me new job but a was wrong, it didn't suit hir atall. Ivery time a landed in the door she started hurlin' abuse at me. What time de ye call this, me lady, an' what kine of a fool de ye think ye'r makin' of me, an' who was that out there in that car way ye, an' de ye know the kine of a name ye'r gettin' this house?

Soon me da started te shout at me too, tellin' me a should lave the job because they weren't payin' me enough money. A didn't want te lave the woman before she had hir wain because a knew that she was lonely, but the longer a stayed in the job, the worse me ma's rantin' got. For over a fortnight the only wink of sleep a got was when a was sittin' in an armchair listenin' te the woman a worked for tellin' me for the hundreth time the history of wan of hir frocks, or how she come by a particular bottle of perfume, or of the night she met hir husband for the first time who wasn't really so bad lookin' atall before hes hair went.

A wasn't outa the convent a month before a was wishin' mesel' back in it so as a could be free from me ma's tormentin'. The Reverent Mother, way all the penances at hir disposal, had niver been able te get te me. A certin part of me had always foun' comedy in hir ridiculousness, especially at the many times when she grew elated an' toul the novices about the joy she would feel wheniver hir body would be released at last, leavin' hir free te rush victoriously inte the arms of the waitin' bridegroom. A could niver stap mesel' thinkin' while lookin' at hir, that maybe the poor bridegroom wouldn't be half as pleased way hes prize as she would be way hirs, because she had a face that looked for all the worl' like the freshly plucked arse of a goose. Nivertheless, a could fine nothin' in me ma's behaviour te amuse me. A wasn't able te view hir as a figure of fun, even when a badly needed te, because a loved hir a suppose.

Two days before the woman a worked for had hir

te give me somethin' for it. They said they had some more questions te ask. A stapped answerin' their questions te see if it would make them change their tune but it didn't stap them writin' in their book. After that a come te the conclusion that the only way te get anythin' for the pain was te really convince them that a was mad. A set there for a wheen of minutes tryin' te think what would do it an' a hit on a great idea. Then a said te them in a big loud voice, a say, a said, this will probably come as a great surprise te all of you, but it just has te be said, a have a father, who has an arse, that doesn't seem te know the first fuckin' thing about how te shoot rabbits.

A hushed silence descended then upon me white coat captors who exchanged pityin' glances way wan another but outa common human dasency an' compassion avoided te look at me. The first person te get hes wits back after me speech was the bald head doctor. He said te wan of the nurses, Nurse Doherty, take this patient an' prepare hir for bed an' give hir two of these as soon as possible. He wrote out a prescription an' handed it te hir. Nurse Doherty took charge of me arm an' asked another woman te assist hir an' they led me aff down a corridor carefully, an eighteen-year-old geriatric.

A was brought inte a bathroom where they started te take aff me clothes. A tried te give them a han' but they couldn't hear of such a thing an' got me te sit still te let them do iverythin' themsel's. They took very great care way me stockin's, makin' sure not te ladder or snag them way their nails. They put me on te a weighin' scales an' said a was six stone nine. When they measured me height a was five feet tall, an' they wrote it all inte a book.

They got some lotion an' put it on me hair te kill the moudies that a didn't have. Then they put me in a bath an' washed me an' took me out an' dried me an' dressed me in a nightgown that looked like a nun's petticoat. They brought me te a bed that looked like an ordinary enough bed till they put me in it an' it turned out to be a cot. A allowed that it must be true what they say about iverythin' comin' te those that stan' an' wait, even the privilege of sleepin' in a cot.

As soon as a was put in me cot the nurses give me some tablets an' a drink of water an' not long after that a fell inte a deep sleep. Wheniver a was a wee wain me ma used te worry about me in case a would smother in the night because a took te sleepin' on me face. Even after a was grown she used te come inte me room in the middle of the night an' wake me up te make sure that a wasn't dead, so a was very surprised indeed when a wakened up an' foun' that a had been sleepin' on me back. Then a minded where a was an' a noticed that the pain was gone an' that a was thirsty an' that somebody was houlin' me han'.

It took me a long time te get me eyes te open for they were stuck shut, an' when a managed te pull the lids apart there was wile big commotion an' people in white coats started te gather roun' me cot that had turned back inte a bed again, te quiz me about who a was. A looked te see if it was me ma or da that was houlin' me han' an' it was neither of them but me best frien' who was a priest.

Wheniver a looked at him the rarest thing happened. He said, de ye know who a am, Ann? A said, what are ye talkin' about, ye eegit ye, ye know rightly a know who ye are, ye'r Frank Gilligan c.c. of our parish. He started te cry an' a felt wile bad about hurtin' hes feelin's so a said a was sorry te him an' he wasn't an eegit atall. But he kept on cryin' an' then laughin' an' cryin' an' laughin' an' sayin', thank god, thank god.

The nurses tried te get him te come away from me bedside, tellin' him that he needed a rest. Nurse Doherty asked me did a know what day it was an' a allowed that it must be the day after a went inte the mental, so a said, is it Sunday? She said, naw, it's Wednesday. Then she toul me that a had been asleep all the time since a come in an' that Frank niver left me side since nine a-clock on Sunday night, except for half an hour ivery mornin' te say mass in a wee room just beside the ward. She said he must be dead beat. When a looked at him again a realised that he was wan of the few people a had iver met who wasn't just pretendin' hes way through life, he really did practise what he preached, an' a was wile proud of him allthegether.

After a'd had a drink of water a felt wile hungry an' toul the nurses so. They said that all the meals were over for the day but they would see what they could fine. About an hour later they brought me a cup of tay an' some toast that had been left over since breakfast time an' an egg that wasn't boiled atall but only heated, so a couldn't ate it. Nurse Doherty come along way two more tablets for me but a toul hir a didn't need them because the pain in me neck was gone. She said a had te take them because they were prescribed. A wheen of minutes after a took them a went to sleep again.

A woke up in the mornin' hungry an' a nurse toul me that a wasn't te get any breakfast because a was down for E.C.T. an' it needed a general anaesthetic. A toul hir that a was down for nothin' because a was goin' home. She said there was no way that a was goin' home till a was well an' that me ma had signed the necessary documents givin' them full permission te give me any treatment that was needed.

After a got the E.C.T. a couldn't mine me own name. The only thing a knew was that a was hungry. When they give me tay an' toast a started te feel tired, then a minded about things called beds an' wanted te lie down on wan of them so they let me. Wheniver they woke me up again te take me down te the dinin' room for me dinner, a minded that a had a ma an' da

99

but a couldn't mine where a knew them from or where they lived or anythin' else about them.

Frank come te see me after a had finished aten an' a minded who he was too an' toul him that a had been given an operation an' couldn't mine very much about anythin', only what me name was an' that a had a ma an' da livin' somewhere. He looked wile worried for a while an' then he started te cry an' a minded that he had been cryin' before after a wakened up. Then a minded about the pain in the back of me neck an' about bein' in the mental.

Frank toul me te get ready te come straight home te me ma an' da that minute but the doctors said that he had no right te take me out because me ma had give them full permission te give me any treatment that was needed an' they were legally responsible for me. They stayed legally responsible for me for another five weeks, an' in that time they give me E.C.T. three times a week, an' twenty tablets ivery day, an' lotion te kill the moudies that a didn't have in me hair, ivery Saturday mornin'.

A couldn't stap them givin' me the E.C.T. because it was legal, but a cried ivery day they done it te me an' a pleaded way them not te, because it was horrible. It was like a recurrin' nightmare that ye couldn't remember wheniver ye woke up but when ye were havin' it ye knew it had all happened before. They give ye an injection in the bed in the mornin' that made ye feel thirsty. Then they put ye inte a stretcher way wheels on it an' pushed ye te the treatment room. Wheniver they got ye there ye could see other patients, men an' weemen of all ages an' sexes lyin' side by side in various states of undress. Some waitin' te have it done, some lyin' grey-faced an' spent after, an' others in the process of the treatment way things like headphones strapped te their skulls, sendin' electric currents inte their brains te induce epilectic-type convulsions that turned the body rigid for some seconds' agony that the general anaesthetics couldn't dull, their mouths clamped open way some apparatus te stap them from swallyin' their tongues. After it was over the only thing ye could feel was a desperate headache an' a ferocious desire for tay an' marmalade an' toast.

Wheniver a was in hospital for nearly six weeks me da come te see me. He started te talk about ordinary things like how the turf was dryin' in the moss an' how it wouldn't be very long till he brought hes first load home. As he was sittin' there talkin' a started te mine more things about him because it was Sunday afternoon an' a hadn't had any E.C.T. since Friday mornin'. A was lookin' at hes han's while he was talkin' (me da has these wee toy han's that look like they niver done a day's work in their lives), tryin' hard to remember what kine of work he done, but the only thing a could mine about him was that he had been in jail.

A started te quiz him then about the jail an' what he done te be put in it an' how long he got. Me da become wile angry an' toul me that he had done nothin' te get put in jail, an' had niver appeared in a court of law in hes life, an' that he had got locked up because he was an Irishman, an' that he could of walked free be signin' himsel' out at any time if he hadn't had hes principles. A toul me da that a didn't have no principles but a still couldn't walk free, so a asked him was it because a was an' Irishwoman that a had been locked up. Me da toul me that a was talkin' nonsense for a wasn't locked up atall, but a toul him that a was, because they wouldn't let me out. A said te me da, a suppose it's agen your principles te sign me out, so he said that it wasn't, an' he brought me home.

Before we left the mental the doctors give me da all the tablets of the day an' warned him that if he iver wanted te see me well again he would have te see te it that a took them ivery day. As soon as we got home, he give all the tablets te me ma an' toul hir that he'd had the strictest instructions from the doctors an' nurses that a was te take them ivery day if a was iver goin' te get better.

A toul me ma an' da that a was goin' te take no more tablets because the pain in me neck was gone. Me ma an' da toul me that it was nonsense a was talkin' because our family doctor toul them that a had no pain in me neck atall. A said te them that the doctor was aff hes own bloody head because when a had a pain, he wouldn't give me anythin' for it, sayin' that it didn't exist, an' now that it was gone, he was busy stuffin' me full of tablets that a didn't need, tryin' to pretend there was somethin' wrong with ME.

For six weeks after a got outa the mental me ma stood over me four times a day an' made me swally the tablets down in the way she had been instructed. At the en' of that time, a was still five feet tall, but me weight had gone up te nine stone. Ivery week me ma took me te the doctor te get a new supply of tablets. Each time we visited him he give the same answer te all me ma's anxious questions about me condition. These things take time, ye know, Mrs McGlone, Rome wasn't built in a day. An' each time he finished writin' out hes perscription he patted wee me on the head.

Roun' this time a begin te feel desperate because a could see visions of me livin' at home for the rest of me life, apprenticed te me ma as a full-time tablet ater who would niver be able te get hirsel' a job because she was only able te stay awake for two hours at a time. A couldn't even concentrate on me hobbies. Goin' for walks an' talkin' te people tired me out, the idea of climbin' a tree filled me way horror, but worst of all, a wasn't able te read two lines in a book before the words got muddled up an' crossed inte wan another. But a'm not a wan that stays desperate for very long about anythin' so a soon started te look for a way outa me dilemma.

Te begin' way, the first thing a had te do was stap takin' the tablets, which was a lot easier said than done, for me ma was determined te make me better an' she wasn't the kine of woman that took the risk of trustin' anybody, especially a body that was mental, so she always made sure that a swallied the tablets down be checkin' in underneath me tongue, for the doctor had warned hir that mental cases were liable te cheat in order te prevent other people from helpin' them.

The only way roun' the problem was for me te swally the tablets when she give them te me, an' then te bring them back up again be pushin' me fingers down me throat an' makin' mesel' throw up wheniver me ma wasn't lookin'. After a had been doin' this for a wheen of weeks, a was feelin' more like mesel' again, an' a begin' te act like a real eighteen-year-oul, givin' me ma back cheek an' askin' hir what she thought a was, a bloody wain, sittin' aroun' an' lettin' hir stuff me full of stupid tablets.

Me ma was wile disappointed allthegether an' toul the doctor that a seemed more mesel' again because a had got the oul lip back. The doctor smiled an' said that a was certinly lookin' a lot brighter, an' hadn't he toul me that if a kept on takin' the tablets a would get well again? A said te the doctor that seein' as a was so improved, a would like te stap takin' the tablets. He said that if a did that, a would soon go back te the way a was before a started takin' them, an' a agreed.

He toul me that a would have te keep on takin' the tablets for years, if not for the rest of me life. A lost me temper way the doctor an' toul him that he might intend te carry on drinkin' for years, if not for the rest of hes life, but a wouldn't listen te hes oul baloney any longer, or take any more of hes tablets. Me ma hit me a clout on the ear for insultin' the doctor, an' a decided that that would be the last chance a would give hir te hit me, so a went outa the surgery an' bought mesel' a newspaper an' started te look up jobs an' flats in Belfast.

The paper was full of jobs an' flats, but a had te stay at home for another month te save enough money te pay for a fortnight's rent in advance an' te live on till a got me first pay packet. Me ma was in a wile shockin' state allthegether when she foun' out that a didn't want te live way hir anymore for she had got used te havin' me about the house again, but when she couldn't fine any way of stappin' me from goin' she went te a frien' of hirs an' borrowed fifty poun' te give te me, in case a was iver stuck.

Chapter 6

Wheniver a landed at the in Belfast there were two other girls livin' in it. Wan of them was a girl a knew when a was a wain. She was the daughter of a man who had become notorious in our town twenty years earlier for comin' home from work wan night an' tellin' hes son of three that he had seen a bird's nest in a bush five miles away. The minute the wee boy heard about this, he would do nothin' but bawl an' kick an' scream till hes da promised te take him te see the nest for himsel'. As soon as the man was finished hes dinner, he got the wee boy dressed up in hes coat an' cap an' headed aff way him be the han' an' niver stapped walkin' till he reached the bird's nest. When word spread roun' our town about this, people started te say that the man was a bit simple, for if he wasn't, they argued, why on earth didn't he pacify the wain be takin' it out te the nearest hedge an' showin' it the first thing that looked like a bird's nest, instead of trapsin' aff on a ten mile roun' trip for nothin'.

This man's daughter was the same age as me an' she was beautiful. She had a steady boyfrien' that took hir out three times a week, an' two other boyfrien's who took hir out on the nights hir real boyfrien' went te night classes. Hir name was Peggy, an' she said she believed in enjoyin' hirsel' as much as possible because she was only goin' te be young wance. A suppose she musta thought te hirsel' that people couldn't have any fun after they reached a certin age.

A don't know whether the other girl who lived in the flat was beautiful or not because a niver got a good enough look at hir. She kept hir face hid away all the time behine a heavy mask of make-up. Hir eyes were always shaded way false eye-lashes that were so sharp an' spiky an' dangerous lookin' that ye couldn't risk goin' too close te hir in case ye got yersel' impaled on them. Hir name was Cassie, an' hir ma had threw hir outa hir own house because she kept on havin' wains an' hir not married. She wasn't allowed te keep hir wains (three) so she give them all te the nazareth nuns in case the neighbours foun' out about them an' thought hir family were a whole crowd of oul low-come-downs.

Hir ma was the president of the local presidium of the Legion of Mary, an' she had a son called Gerrard Majella after the patron saint of mothers, who was a priest. He beat Cassie up an' called hir a dirty oul whore ivery time he met hir. Cassie was wan year ouler than Peggy an' me, an' the minute a landed at the flat, she took a great interest in tryin' te get me smartened up so a would be able te go way hir to the Flamingo Ballroom an' have the time of me life.

Cassie soon begin te fix me up way blin' dates, middle-aged businessmen in expensive suits way gold cufflinks an' tie pins, who looked for all the worl' like husbands out on the town for a good time while their wives were safely tucked away in hospital havin' their fourteenth wain. She always brought the blin' dates roun' te our flat, an' a had te get rid of them be tellin' them that if they liked te hang aroun' for a while, a would call the polis — none of them hung aroun'.

The day after a landed in Belfast a applied for three jobs an' a was delighted way mesel' when a got a letter a wheen of days later tellin' me te start work as a machinist in a factory five miles outside Belfast on the followin' Monday mornin' at half-past eight. The advertisement said that after workin' there for six weeks ye could be makin' up te forty pounds a week, an' a allowed that that wasn't te be sneezed at.

When a got on the bus te go te work on the Monday mornin' at a quarter te eight, a bought a weekly ticket an' set back all pleased way mesel' for gettin' straightened out so soon. The bus arrived at the factory gate at two minutes te the half hour, an' a asked directions aff wan of the other girls. She was wile civil allthegether an' she toul me that there was a very friendly atmosphere in the factory, an' the girls were just like wan big happy family, an' a would fine that a would settle in way no bother. She wished me all the best when she left me outside the supervisor's office an' a thought that a was aff te a very fine start.

The supervisor fitted me up way an overall (the smallest she could find, a had gone back te bein' small woman again after a stapped takin' tablets), then she took me along te the machine room te show me where te work. As soon as she opened the machine room door it wasn't just the din that hit me. In fact a hardly noticed the noise atall way the shock a got when a seen the cut of the place.

It could be said te have had a family atmosphere a suppose, dependin' that is on which particular family it was ye happened te belong te. A took a deep breath an' thanked almighty god for the first time in me life for givin' me the wee screwed up protestant face that so grieved me ma an' a smiled at them all as if a had just been given the most wonderful birthday surprise.

FUCK THE POPE. DEATH TO ALL PAPISTS. LONG LIVE PROTESTANT ULSTER. THE ONLY GOOD CATHOLIC IS A DEAD CATHOLIC. GOD SAVE THE QUEEN. ULSTER IS BRITISH. GOD SAVE KING BILLY. REMEMBER THE BOYNE an' things like that were written on banners an' hung wan after the other for the full length of the factory. A allowed that if a knew what was good for me a would act the part of a real loyal protestant for the rest of that day.

Things went smoothly enough while a was sittin' at me machine that was nicely decked out in red white an' blue buntin' way two wee union jacks that were flutterin' happily away in the gentle breeze of an overhead fan. A thought te mesel' that if a was able te keep me terrible secret all the way through lunch break a just might be lucky enough te get mesel' outa the place in the evenin' in much the same shape as a went inte it in the mornin',

As soon as the bell sounded for the start of the lunch hour all the girls come crowdin' over roun' my machine way big wide welcomin' smiles on their faces te take me aff te the canteen. They were all wile civil, an' wheniver they heard the news that a come from our town (that is a ninety five per cent catholic town) they were wile shockin' sympathetic te me allthegether an' said that they could see why a wanted te lave a hole like that. A agreed that it was indeed a terrible place, an' a toul them that a was wile, wile glad te see the back of it.

Te begin way, a had te be very careful not te say the wrong thing in case they twigged on that a was catholic, so a limited mesel' te repeatin' verbatim what the dreadful catholics from our town said about us protestants, an' only repeatin' some of the better known anti-catholic slogans, but as me confidence increased, a got te enjoy the part a was playin' so much, that a become more excessive an' outspoken than any of the others in me scathin' criticism an' condemnation of fuckin' popish scum. (God was a glad that me ma was outa ear-shot.)

The day passed aff so well that be the time a was finished work in the evenin' a had made arrangements te meet three of the girls at eight that night, at an address a remembered from lookin' up flats in the paper before a come te live in Belfast. They were plannin' te take me te a big do in an orange hall where some wile shockin' big important high-up man be the name of the Reverent Ian Paisley was comin' te make a speech. A toul them that a had niver had the pleasure of meetin' him before an' they assured me that a was in for a treat.

Nixt mornin' a didn't go te work. At ten a-clock a phoned up the manager te say that a wasn't comin' back. He asked me was a catholic be any chance. A toul him that a was. He said he could see how a job in that factory would be completely unsuitable for a catholic girl, but he'd thought that a was a protestant because a had applied or he would of warned me. He said he was an Englishman an' couldn't understand all this catholic-protestant carry-on.

He allowed it was a pity that a had te lave because of the good impression a had made on iverybody the day before. He commended me for me ability te bluff me way outa a very dangerous corner an' said he was very sorry to be losin' me. Then he toul me that he had been workin' there for less than a year himsel' an' he hoped te be movin' back te hes native Newcastle te take up a similar post soon, before the crazy weemen in the factory foun' out that he was a catholic too. A said to him that he had no need te worry about that because hes name was a very protestant name, an' he laughed at me an' said he would niver know atall what te make of the Irish.

In the post nixt mornin' a got a letter from him full of all the apologies of the day way me card stamped an' a month's wages te help me out till a found another job. The letter said that if a wanted a reference from him he would be only too willin' te give me wan or he would do anythin' else in hes power te help me. A allowed that a might be better aff without the reference because a couldn't imagine what he could say te impress a future employer about a body who only stuck a job for wan day.

For a wheen of days after that a had a quare good time te mesel' spendin' all the money a made from me protestant day's work. At the en' of the nixt week a got mesel' another job as a slicer an' seller of bacon an' all kines of coul meat an' pies in a supermarket that was just aroun' the corner from me flat. The man who owned the supermarket took me on for a week's trial first te see if a was any good because he had niver give a job of bacon slicer te a girl before. He foun' out that a could do it very well, an' he was delighted way himsel' because he only had te give me half the pay a man would get, so be the en' of the week he made me permanent.

A was workin' on the bacon slicer for eight weeks when the man said he was very pleased way me so he give me a rise. A was all delighted way this so a decided te buy mesel' a new coat way some of the money a had saved up for a rainy day because a allowed the way things were lookin' for me, no rainy day was iver likely te come my way again. As soon as a got mesel' this new coat, a started te wear the wan that had been me Sunday best te work.

After a left the convent a became a lay person again, so me ma made me retake the pledge te abstain for life from all alcoholic beverages, for the greater glory an' honour of god, for the conversion of excessive drinkers, an' in case a iver got a taste for the booze, because there is no knowin' what depths of depravity a spoilt nun is liable te stoop te disgrace hir ma.

Well, when a took up the pledge again, a pinned me pioneer badge on te the lapel of me then best Sunday coat. It was because a forgot te change it on te me new coat that a landed at work in the supermarket, the week after a got me rise, way a pioneer pin danglin' from me lapel, for the first, an' as it turned out, the last time.

Ivery day at lunch time, the wife of the man that owned the supermarket landed te have lunch in the office way hir husband te try te minimise hes chances of idlin' in the company of attractive young girls. Wheniver she would finish aten hir calorie-controlled lunch of grated carrot, lettuce, an' two carefully weighed ounces of whole meal bread, she would set out on a gran' tour of inspection of the supermarket floor, te cast disdainful glances over all hir social inferiors, staff an' customers alike. She was a woman that nature hadn't been kind te but niver the less, she was very much in awe of hirsel' since a time ten years earlier when she got hirsel' a pass certificate in education from a third rate teacher trainin' college somewhere in the north of England.

Imagine my delight when such a gran' lady as hirsel' should stap right beside me bacon slicer an' take a great interest in examinin' me second best coat. A was beginnin' te question me judgement in not keepin' this obviously interestin' garment for a Sunday when she called out for hir husband te come at once an' tell hir who the owner of me coat was. Hir husband was a wee man called Alex who sweated a lot when she was about, an' said, yes dear, quite right dear, te hir, no matter what she said te him.

De ye know who this coat belongs te, Alex? dear demanded, pointin' at me nearly Sunday best. Yes dear, Alex answered, sweatin' more than usual. Well, who Alex? Ann, dear. De ye know that Ann dear is a catholic? Well, my dear, dear, stuttered Alex. Sack hir this minute, shouted dear. A dear, dear, a can't do that, dear, said Alex. Can't do what? demanded dear. This is mother's business, dear, an' mother knows that Ann is a catholic, dear, a can't go sackin' mother's staff, dear. If ye want te see me or the twins again, Alex, you will get rid of hir instantly, understand? Yes, dear, indeed, dear, Alex whimpered, as he trotted outa the supermarket an' down the street after the angry dear.

Alex didn't look me in the face again for the rest of that day even though he had always been most civil te me since the day a first went te work for him − or as it turned out, much te my surprise, mother. Mother niver behaved like she owned the business atall, because she wanted hir only son te know what it felt like te be boss somewhere a suppose.

At the en' of that day, wheniver a had finished washin' up me bacon slicer, mother come over te me an'

111

took me be the han' an' led me up stairs te the office where Alex an' hes dear dined daily. She made me tay an' give me a cream bun an' toul me she was sorry she would have te let me go. She explained te me that Alex thought he was lucky te have such a good wife as dear, who was not like hes last wife, that had run aff way a bus driver te Liverpool, an' took hes only son way hir, niver te be heard of again.

Mother said that nobody was perfect, an' it was just wan of them things that dear didn't like catholics. Then mother said that in the oul days, when they had been buildin' up their business, hir an' Alex's da, god rest hes soul this day, had always employed catholics because they foun' them te be much more conscientious an' far less likely te be dippin' their han's inte the till than their own sort. A said te mother that it sure was a great comfort for me te know that.

Well, a was wile sorry indeed for havin' bought mesel' that new coat an' a decided niver te risk doin' anythin' that silly again, for if there was wan thing a had learned up till then, it was niver te make the same mistake twice.

For a couple of weeks after that a made me livin' be signin' on the dole because a had no particular desire te change me religion for the protestant faith as a allowed that it wouldn't please me ma much, an' a did mean te go on visits te hir sometimes, like Christmas, or Easter, or if for any reason atall a iver happened te fine mesel' destitute.

When a went te the dole te sign on for the third week in a row, they toul me that they had a job that would suit me down te the groun'. It was housekeepin' for a priest that lived in a town about ten miles away. (Ex-nuns are highly regarded as just the right kine of people te skivvy for priests.) A set aroun' for a wheen of days thinkin' about it before a come te the conclusion that maybe the divil ye know is better than the divil ye don't know after all, so a went back te the dole office an' toul them a would try it for a while.

An interview was arranged, an' the very nixt day the parish priest landed at me flat half an hour early, te try te catch me on the hop. Me two flat mates hid behine the bathroom door te hear how a parish priest interviewed a body for a job, because they allowed that they were niver likely te have any personal experience of the kine.

He was a big grey man of about forty-five years oul way a couple of heavy chins an' a very wide wasteline. He was wearin' a pair of shoes way a hole in the right toe an' wan of the tattiest suits of clothes a body could iver hope te avoid seein'. He took a great shine te me allthegether, for a was on me best dignified behaviour, oozin' refinement an' religious decorum as taught te me be the good nuns.

The money he offered me was very paltry indeed, but a thought be lookin' at the cut of hes clothes that he must be wan of them saintly priests that a body hears about from time te time, who give away their last penny te the poor an' needy so a didn't feel it right te refuse. He asked me te start work right away because it was confirmation day in hes parish in less than a fortnight an' the bishop was comin' te stay overnight.

A packed all me things in a suitcase, an' he took me along te hes parish. The first thing that he done when we landed there was bring me aroun' the town te introduce me te all the people in the shops where a was te do hes buyin' for him.

Very young, wan oul doll said te another after lookin' me well over way studied disapproval, not the thing te be livin' way a priest atall. She looks all right te me, remarked another oul wan who was sizin' me up from a different angle, not like some of these mini-skirted hussies that are goin' about nowadays way their arses bare.

Deflated a was after all this tourin' when we landed at the parochial house. It was a big white mansion of a place, sittin' up aloofly in its own well tended groun's. He drove aroun' te the back of the house in hes wee beat up mini an' opened up the garage door. A looked in an' seen a gleamin' new Rover so a said te him, a say, that's nice. He made no reply but there was no mistakin' hes answer, it was as plain as the nose on hes face (the nose on hes face was very plain indeed, way a big bulbus red en' on it), he didn't want te be atall familiar way a servant.

As soon as a got outa the car he went roun' te the boot an' opened it up an' toul me te get me suitcase out an' take it te the kitchen an' wait for further instructions. Well, as a mentioned before, a couple of times, my family are not famous for growin', so a'm not really built te be cartin' heavy loads, especially suitcases crammed full of books which unfortunately enough are the only kine of suitcases a like te take anywhere way me, so a asked him te help me te carry it.

Wheniver a was leavin' me flat in Belfast, he had gallantly hulked me suitcase down three flights of stairs way the pious praise of me lan'lady ringin' in hes ears tellin' him what a gentleman he was, but now he didn't seem so keen. If ye fine it too difficult te manage be yersel' ye may ask the gardener te assist, he said shortly, an' stalked aff, lavin' me te open it there on the groun' an carry the contents, armfuls at a time, inte the kitchen.

A didn't see him again for half an hour, but a heard him on the phone makin' calls te all hes frien's tellin' them that he had at last managed te get a housekeeper, an' that she had excellent references. He went on te start apologisin' for me te them, sayin' that he hoped they didn't think a was a bit inexperienced, ye see, he explained, she is quite young, middle-twenties about.

Well, a was fuckin' furious when a heard him tryin' te pass me aff as an' oul woman just te suit hes prejudice, but a blamed mesel' partly for not wearin' the proper mini-skirt an' a resolved te set the matter straight at me

114

earliest opportunity.

At last he landed in the kitchen an' started upbraidin' me for havin' what he described as me personal belongin's sittin' in wee piles all over the place. A toul him a was waitin' te fine out where me room was, an' he said a should have made mesel' busy in the mean time be gettin' on way me work. (He was probably referrin' te the big pile of dirty dishes that looked like they niver seen water in fifty years.)

Now, needless te say, a had gone clean aff him be this time, but because it was a wile long walk back te Belfast, an' a was tired, an' a had nothin' better te do anyway, a decided te stay on way him for a while an' give him a good run for hes money, two poun' ten shillin's a week.

He brought me roun' the house then te show me me duties, an' a was not a bit surprised te learn that he had only been tryin' te con me inte thinkin' he was poor when he landed te interview me in hes oul raggy suit an' wile holy shoes. He had a wardrobe room nixt te hes bedroom, an' after he had finished tellin' me how important it was te him that hes bed be changed ivery day, an' showin' me how te make it way hospital corners, only not tucked in at hes feet, an' warnin' me how, when he got inte hes bed at night, he could always tell right away whether the mattress had been turned an' the bed completely stripped since the last time he slept in it, an' showin' me how te turn on hes electric blanket at night (two hours after me usual bedtime), he took me inte hes wardrobe room te show me how te look after hes clothes.

As a had niver been in a wardrobe room before (or come te think of it, since), me eyes nearly popped outa me head when a seen the vast array of gear that he kept. Even the woman a had worked for after a come outa the convent didn't possess such a fine stock as he. Hes priestly vestments of all the different colours were in wan wardrobe, an' another wan was full of all hes shirts. A third wardrobe hel' nothin' but hes suits. Not all of them were black. Some of them were nice coloured wans that he musta wore on holidays or wheniver he went down te the other side of the border te pick up a loose woman, a suppose. (People in the north of Ireland believe that the weemen on the other side of the border have looser morals than the wans in the north an' people in the south think the opposite is true.)

Wheniver he was finished exposin' all hes wardrobes te me an' showin' me through hes drawers that were full of nothin' but hankies an' collars an' ties an' socks an' vests an' knickers, he showed me how te lay out hes fresh clothes for him ivery mornin' on a special kine of a clothes horse affair that straddled an electric fan heater that a was te switch on half an hour before he was due te get up.

After he was done way all hes instructions about how a was te take care of him, he brought me up te the attic room that had a wee sky-light in the roof an' holy martyrs pictures pasted on the walls an' a hospital bed way wan blanket on it, an' started te list out another set of rules that a was te folly in relation te me own humble quarters.

He toul me te keep me room clean an' tidy an' well aired at all times an' niver te entertain no visitors in it, or smoke cigarettes, or drink alcohol, or do anythin' whatsoiver that might bring disgrace inte the house of a parish priest. A assured him that he could depend on me, an' he departed, leavin' me alone te plan me strategy.

A have niver been a great wan for takin' drastic action agen anybody no matter how much they appear te deserve it, not for any moral reasons, let me hasten te add, but simply because a believe that such action can often back-fire on the perpetrator, so a sadly decided that a must act strictly within the letter of the law.

The first thing a planned te do was take up smokin' an' drinkin' right away but a knew that these were both expensive hobbies so a decided te smoke hes cigarettes an' drink hes whiskey te save mesel' a wheen of bob. Then a made out a list of all the people from our town, frien's an' neighbours an' even relatives, who had emigrated an' were livin' in far away lonely places like Australia an' America, an' who would be delighted beyond all measure way a nice long phone call from dear oul Ireland tellin' them how they were missed an' all sorts of lies like that. A started te get ready for bed then, when me mine, for some unknown reason of its own, begin te turn te bishops.

The nixt mornin' when a woke up way a headache a wasn't sure whether it was the smokin' or the drinkin' that had brought it on, or only just the pure excitement a was feelin' at the thought of how a was goin' te enjoy me new job.

The parish priest, after tellin' me aff for all the things a had done wrong, like not waitin' te be spoke te first before speakin' mesel', an' not standin' up wheniver he entered the kitchen, an' not servin' from the right an' clearin' away from the left or whichiver way it's supposed te be for a can't right mine, an' not puttin' out a butter knife, an' not puttin' the jam on a dish, an' the milk in a jug, an' not settin' out the cutlery right, an' not cuttin' the crusts aff hes bread, an' not givin' him a serviette, an' not puttin' a tay cosy on hes tay pot, an' not callin' tay tea, an' not bowin' me head down right in hes presence, an' not walkin' about way soft shoes so as te make no noise, an' not ironin' hes mornin' paper before givin' it te him te read, an' not puttin' out a note for the milkman tellin' him how much milk a wanted, an' not makin' him hes supper the night before, an' not turnin' on hes electric blanket half an hour before he was due te go te hes bed (an' two hours after a was due te go te mine), an' not rakin' out the coals of the fire at night, an' not lightin' the fire in the mornin', an' not layin' out hes clothes an' turnin' on hes heater in hes wardrobe room, an' not polishin' hes shoes, started te brief me on what was needed te be done for hes lordship the bishop's arrival on the followin' Saturday week.

A took all hes instructions in me stride that day, an' as soon as he was finished them a headed aff te the butchers shop te pick up the roast of beef that he had ordered for hes dinner. When a got back the house was empty so a stuck the roast in the oven an' made the first of me long distant calls te Australia. It was te a girl that a used te know when we were still wains, a sister of Peggy that a shared the flat in Belfast way, an' when a got through te hir number they thought a was callin' from somewhere near because a toul them that it was all right for hir te take hir leisure comin' out of the shower as a had plenty of time te wait. After we had been confabbin' on the phone for half an hour she asked me how long a had been out in Australia an' a toul hir that a hadn't really arrived there yet but way, the way things were lookin' for me at that moment, it probably wouldn't be long before a would be transported.

Hes reverence landed in for hes dinner at wan a-clock an' a toul him that he was outa luck because the dinner was over, an' the nixt time the dinner was ordered at twelve a would appreciate it very much if he would come an' ate it after me slavin' over a hot stove all mornin'. Hes face turned red an' then white an' he clenched hes fists an' said te me, how dare ye speak in that manner te the parish priest. A nearly toul him what a thought of hes gallantry, parish priest or no parish priest, but a stapped mesel' short because a thought it might be better for me te houl back me hackles for the time bein'.

Durin' the nixt week a become a real model of an ideal wee priest's housekeeper, stayin' up late at night te attend te all hes orders an' gettin' up at the crack of dawn te set hes clothes out an' turn on hes heater in hes wardrobe room an' light hes fire te have it nice an' ready for him te come down te.

All the oul weemen that a met in the parish toul me how he was a new man since a come te look after him. They said that a was just the right kine of a good goer that was needed te run the parochial house. Wan pious oul doll who swore that the parish priest was a walkin' saint gave me earnest details about all the terrible trials an' tribulations he'd had all through the years way housekeepers that didn't know their proper place, god almighty forgive them, she said, for they'll have little luck, an' a agreed.

It was true what they said about him lookin' better for he was a wile relieved man for the first time in years way a house runnin' nice an' smoothly te show the bishop an' no oul moody spinster of the usual sort te have te contend way inte the bargain.

There was just wan wee cloud on hes horizon, but not bein' an allthegether stupid man, he musta put it down largely te childish stubbornness on my part when he decided te wait till after the bishop's visit te iron the wee matter out, in case hes efforts te achieve total perfection too soon done more harm than good. This wee cloud was there because there was just wan thing he asked that a absolutely refused te do.

The day after a decided te houl back me hackles, the parish priest landed for hes dinner on the stroke of twelve a-clock an' a had iverythin' ready to serve him the minute he set down. It was chicken that day an' a give him the best cut of the bird an' enough te feed a ploughman. The first thing he said te me wheniver a set it down in front of him was, much te me surprise, Ann, for it was the first time he spoke me name since a had started skivvyin' for him, you must not carve the meat yoursel' in future, but bring the joint whole te the table so a can choose what a want mesel'.

A was about te say, yes father, when it occurred te me what he was suggestin', so a said, a can't do that, don't ye know a have me own dinner te get aff it too? That is perfectly all right, said the parish priest te me, you can take it away as soon as a have finished way it. A said, father, am a hearin' ye right? He looked at me way a blank expression for a wheen of minutes before the blood begin te circulate in hes brain again. He musta decided te treat me kindly for after all a was very young an' didn't have much education so he said me name again, Ann, he said, an' it sounded friendly, there are some things that you have not learned yet, an' a'm not criticisin' ye atall because ye are very young, but you must soon learn that there is a right way an' a wrong way to do iverythin'. You must know the proper procedure to follow when servin' at table. From now on you will serve the whole joint, an' do not worry, a will not deprive you. You will be free te ate all ye like after a have had my portion.

A looked at him way an equally blank expression for a wheen of minutes before allowin' mesel' te speak, then a said te him, just te let him see that a could be as polite as he was, father, a said, an' it sounded friendly, a have been livin' on this earth now for the guts of twenty years, an' in that time a have been made te do some very degradin' things, but let me tell ye here an' now, so as ye won't be labourin' under any illusions, a'll be damned before a add te that list be aten your lavins. A suppose me wee speech musta took him be surprise, for he set there lookin' at his plate till a went out inte the kitchen te ate me own dinner.

A allowed that that was the last a would hear about that wee matter but a was wrong for he made wan last try te talk me aroun' te hes way of thinkin' when a come back in te clear the things aff hes table. He said he wanted a word way me an' would a take a seat? A said a would rather stan', thank you. Then he said how very pleased he was way the way a was doin' all the work an' that it was quite remarkable how quick a was at pickin' up the reins, an' the house was lookin' all the better for me efforts, an' would a not please sit down for a moment, so a allowed that seein' as he appeared te be civil a might as well sit down, so a did.

He set there tinkerin' way hes car keys for a wheen of minutes more without sayin' anythin' else, then he said te me, nice an' polite, there's just wan other little matter that a would like te bring up, it's about your strange attitude te the carvin' of the joint.

A stood up again an' a said te him, a have no strange attitudes about anythin', least of all, the carvin' of the joint. A have toul ye that a will give ye whativer part of the meat that ye like best, an' as much of it as ye want, but, a'm doin' the carvin' of it mesel' because there are two of us an' a'm the cook an' a'm not goin', under any circumstances whatsoiver, te ate your lavins.

He set there lookin' dumfounded for a while an' then he said, what is goin' te happen when the bishop comes? That was just the very thing that a didn't want him te know, so a said te him te set hes mine at ease, when the bishop lands, a'll probably be far too busy te be botherin' about a dinner for mesel', a'll just run over te the fish an' chip shop an' get mesel' somethin' quick that day, so a hope you an' the bishop will be able te decide between yersel's which of the two of ye will be doin' the carvin'.

Then a suppose, he said, a should thank the lord for small mercies, but really it is quite irregular for a priest's housekeeper to prevent him from carvin' hes own joint. A said, what de ye mean, irregular? He said, it's not proper. A said, who says it's not proper? He said, it's just bad etiquette, the proper procedure should be followed. Housekeepers should always serve the whole joint an' wait until after to have their own meal. Niver in me whole life have a iver heard anythin' so disgustin', a said, poor priests' housekeepers bein' forced te ate lavins, but a'll tell ye now, a don't believe a word of it. Nice priests wouldn't expect their housekeepers te ate after them. A have a frien' a priest, an' a'm tellin' ye now, he isn't the kine of a man that would expect another human bein' te ate hes lavins, an' a'll prove it be phonin' him up this minute, so a did.

Frank was all delighted when he heard me voice on the phone an' he asked me how Belfast was agreein' way me. A toul him that me an' Belfast had been havin' wee problems in adjustin' te each other's ways so a had moved outa Belfast for a bit an' got mesel' a job as housekeeper te this parish priest. He started te laugh at me. Now if there was wan thing that a liked about Frank more than any other, it was that when he laughed in Derry ye could hear him in Cork, but a was in wan of them moods then when a had little time for laughin'.

When he was finished laughin' at me he said he was goin' te say a prayer for the poor unfortunate parish priest because he obviously didn't know what he was lettin' himsel' in for or he would niver have given me a job as hes housekeeper. Then he started te laugh again. A got mad at him an' said, will ye just cut out the laughin', a have a very serious question te ask ye. He stapped laughin' an' said, sorry Ann, a'v been very thoughtless, are you all right?

A toul him a was gran' only for wan thing, then a explained te him how this parish priest of mine wanted me te ate hes lavins. Frank started te laugh again an' a said a didn't see anythin' funny. He said, Ann, a do believe that you have got yersel' the wrong job. A said, just forget about it bein' the wrong job for a minute an' tell me what ye think of a man that has a body goin' te the butchers in the mornin' for hes beef, an' takin' it home an' spendin' the whole mornin' standin' over a hot stove slavin' te get it ready, an' after a body has done all that, expects hir te ate hes lavins?

Frank wasn't laughin' anymore, in fact a wasn't sure if he was still on the line, so a said te him louder, well tell me what ye think? He said, that's a very, very, now how shall a put it? A said, put it straight. Well, he said, it's a very Ann way of puttin' it. A said, what the hell does that mean? What other way would ye expect me te put it? No, no, he said, don't you iver dare put things in any other way than yer own, for whativer else can be said about you, yer quite unique way of viewin' the worl' is just priceless.

A was gettin' mad at him again because a don't like

122

people wastin' time talkin' roun' things (somethin' he didn't usually do), so a said te him, does Martha ate your lavins? There was a long silence so a said, come on, ye better hurry up an' answer, this call is costin' my parish priest a fortune. Then he said, very carefully, ye see Ann, there are certin norms an' such like that are kept, it's the way things have always been done. A said, are you tryin' te tell me in some arse-about-face way, that you make poor Martha ate your lavins?

Well, Ann, he said, it's not exactly like that. A said, how exactly is it then, tell me how it works? He went on te explain te me how the priest always cut hes own meat aff the joint before sendin' it out te the kitchen for the housekeeper's dinner. Now a was fumin' mad at him an' a said that he was a disgrace an' a wanted te speak te Martha that very minute.

Wheniver Martha come on the phone a asked hir straight out if she ate Frank's lavins. To begin way she didn't seem te know what a was talkin' about. After it come out clear te me that she did in fact ate Frank's lavins, a toul hir niver te dare te do it again because she was the wan that deserved first helpin's after doin' all the slavin'. She said that she was doin' hir job right already an' she knew a lot of other priests' housekeepers an' they always served the priest first for that was the way things were done. Well, a toul hir that if that was the case, then it was clear that things were in damned big need of changin' but she didn't seem te understand me atall, so she put Frank back on the line.

He tried te change the subject but a wouldn't let him, so then he started te say that a was in the wrong job again. A toul him that it was people like him who were in the wrong job, tryin' te make out that they were christians an' at the same time gettin' other people te ate their lavins. Two days after that a got a long letter from Frank, tellin' me how he understood me point of view, an' how right a really was, an' how there were a lot of contradictions in all our lives. A allowed that he wasn't

123

such a bad oul sort after all, an' a nearly forgive him.

A didn't forgive the parish priest a was workin' for though, so in the short time that a was workin' in hes house, he ate what a give him, an' nothin' else. Apart from (what he called, while confabbin' way hes frien's on the telephone) this little idiosyncrasy of mine, a gave him no cause for concern till the mornin' of the Saturday that the bishop was due te arrive.

On the evenin' of the day that a had started workin' in hes house, a decided that of all the days that a could pick for me te go on strike, this would be the best day of all, so on the Friday night a made a nice big pile of sandwiches an' a flask of tay an' stocked me room well up way all the nice wee things of the day that had been bought for the bishop, like a bottle of the best whiskey a body could buy at anybody else's expense, an' set aff te me bed early.

When hes breakfast didn't appear in the mornin' hes reverence set out lookin' for me an' hes search ended up in me bedroom where a was still sleepin' the sleep of the just. De ye know what day it is, he shouted from the doorway, after hammerin' loud enough te waken the dead. A set up in bed startled for a wheen of seconds, then a minded right well what day it was so a said te him, naw. It's Saturday, he said, the bishop will be arrivin' here at three a-clock. God bliss us father, a said, what time is it now? It's nearly ten a-clock he said. God help ye father, a said, sure ye haven't had yer breakfast. Niver mine about breakfast now, a have no time te wait, he said, a'll have a quick coul snack at wan a-clock so in the meantime get up an' start work right away, a nice day ye chose te be lyin' in.

When he went away a poured out a nice wee cup of tay an' propped mesel' up good an' comfortable in the bed an' then set about the real task of the day, readin' banned books that were wrote be a heathen man from Dublin be the name of James Joyce.

It was nearly two a-clock when a heard him comin'

back lookin' for hes coul lunch. A was sittin' up in bed, nibblin' a Garibaldi biscuit (a particular favourite of the bishop's) when he started callin' me name. A stuck the 'Two Gallants' in underneath me pillow when a heard hes footsteps headin' for me door.

Are ye still in bed? he growled. It would seem that way, a said, after first checkin' in underneath the blanket te make sure that a was there. Are ye ill? he asked way scorn, rather than concern. Who? Me? Ill? a said. Naw, a've niver felt better in me life. Then why are ye lyin' in bed? he yelled. Well, a said, ye see father, it's mainly on account of the fact that a have no particular inclination or desire te get up.

The bishop, he screamed in alarm, the bishop, what am a goin' te do way the bishop? O, a said, father, now come on, a don't want you te be goin' away an' gettin' yersel' upset about no oul bishop. Bishops is nothin'. A know that parish priests is often in awe of bishops, an' it's understandable a suppose, but if they knew bishops as well as a know bishops they would pass far less remarks on bishops. Now let me explain bishops te ye father, a said, for ye see, a'm a bit of an expert on bishops. Bishops is no different from you or me father, honest te god. No different from anybody else. Nobody knows that better than me. Ye see father, bishops is so ordinary that a have even had me hair cut be wan. Bishops is nothin' but barbers. That's what bishops is. So now set yersel' at yer ease father, an' have a wee drink of this whiskey, for Christ's sake, before it's all gone.

Chapter 7

A didn't work for the parish priest after that on account of the fact that he give me the sack. The nixt day a was back in Belfast lookin' for a job. Me search, as usual, led me inte wan cul-de-sac after another, so be the en' of a year in which a tried out twenty or more dead-en' jobs, a was fast becomin' the most spectacularly unsuccessful person in the whole of Belfast (that is, if ye don't count the wile shockin' big important high-up man be the name of the Reverent Ian Paisley that a nearly had the pleasure of meetin' on the day a done me protestant day's work).

Paisley was bein' more unsuccessful than me on account of the fact that he was tryin' te stap some students outa Queens University from goin' aroun' way placards demandin' that catholics be given basic civil rights. Ivery time he tried te stap them he only made things worse for himsel' because the newspapers started te come along, an' the TV way their cameras, te take pictures of the students peacefully marchin', an' the wile shockin' big important high-up man shoutin' things at them about the scarlet harlot of Rome, which was wan of the nicer names he had for the pope.

In no time atall the newspaper headlines were fulla nothin' but the protestin' students, an' iverybody in

Northern Ireland was talkin' about them, an' dependin' on whichiver foot they happened te dig way (catholics believe that protestants dig way the wrong foot), sayin' that the students were the divil himsel' or god's only answer te all the problems in the land.

For a wheen of months te begin way the only people that went out marchin' were the students themsel's an' a wheen of the lecturers outa Queens University, but as people listened more te the things that they were sayin', ordinary people started te join in too, for the students were callin' for the en' of discrimination, sayin' that iverybody should have a right te a house an' a vote an' a dasent job regardless of what their religion happened te be. They said that Stormont was a protestant parliament for a protestant people, an' that for fifty years, catholics had been treated as second-class citizens.

Well, when this news broke, a lot of ordinary people were surprised te learn that they had been citizens all their lives, an' not only citizens, but second-class citizens too at that. My god, they were sayin' te wan another, te think that all this time we have been only wan step down from the tap an' didn't know it. They were delighted so they took te the streets in their droves, an' a went way them.

The first march a went te was in Derry on the fifth of October nineteen-sixty-eight. That march turned out not te be a real march atall on account of the fact that as soon as we tried te move aff from the Waterside station, all two thousand of us, we foun' our way blocked be a cordon of polismen lookin' wile fierce. We tried te go by another route, but the polis were there too. The people who organised the march toul us that they didn't want a confrontation way the polis so they just hel' a meetin' instead.

After the meetin' was over wan of the speakers toul us all te go home quietly, but that was aisier said than done because the polis had us herded in on all sides like sheep in a pen on a fair day. Wan of the big head polismen

127

had earlier warned all the weemen an' wains te lave the crowd — because they were plannin' te murder only men that day, a suppose.

Some of the people in the crowd that had come for the march weren't too happy way the polismen for roundin' us up an' makin' us stan' in the wan place without movin', so they said te the polismen, S.S.R.U.C. The polismen weren't too happy way the crowd for bein' there atall so they started te chastise the crowd be beatin' it over the head way big batons.

The crowd begin te bleed an' scream an' tried te run away, but no matter which direction it run away in, it was met be more polismen way batons. As soon as the crowd begin te break through the big throngs of vicious polismen way batons, it was met be a very strange monster indeed, the like of which had niver been seen on the face of Ireland before. This big hideous monster that charged about at seventy miles an hour like a terrible dragon on wheels breathin' out ferocious spurts of ice-coul water way enough force te knock the heaviest man imaginable clean aff hes feet was called Water Cannon, an' the people allowed that it was no mistake atall that it had the same initials as the minister of home affairs because they both bore a strikin' resemblance te wan another.

Later on that night, in a pub in Derry, a new song was wrote an' be the en' of the week half the second-class citizens in the north of Ireland could be heard singin' —

To Derry we went on October the fifth,
To march for our rights,
But o what a mess.
They beat us with batons,
They beat us with fists,
And they hosed us all over with water.

Because a hadn't seen me ma for a long time, an' because it was a long journey back te Belfast, an' because the weather wasn't very hot, an' because a was feelin' terribly tired, an' because a was drooked te the skin, an' because a was droppin' down dead way the hunger, a decided te call in on me family after the march on the way back from Derry.

Me ma couldn't have been more pleased te see me if she hada tried, because just before a landed in the door she had been watchin' the news on television an' she had seen me bein' grabbed be a big hefty polisman way a cudgel in hes han' an' a look of murder on hes face, so she thought a was a goner. After she was finished huggin' an' kissin' me an' examinin' me te make sure that no bits of me were broke or missin', a had te explain te hir how it was that a had managed te escape from the big hefty polisman way the cudgel in hes han' an' the look of murder on hes face be tellin' hir that the big hefty polisman way the cudgel in hes han' an' the look of murder on hes face had niver had a hoult of me atall but only the back of me coat that had got me inte all the trouble before in Belfast way dear an' Alex an' mother, an' how it was that a had managed te run away from him, an' the coat, glad te be rid of the both of them, an' how a hoped he enjoyed ownin' that coat more than a did.

A didn't have a job te go back te at the time so a decided that seein' as me ma's reception was so cordial a might as well stay on at home for a while. Very soon a become a fulltime listener an' looker at the news on the wireless an' television, an' an expert switcher from wan channel te another wheniver somethin' interestin' was announced, in the hope of hearin' it all over again on the other side.

Nearly ivery night, the television studios would be packed full of all the wile big important high-up people of the day, sittin' discussin' the latest developments, an' this wee student girl outa Cookstown be the name of Bernadette Devlin, would be sittin' up there beside them all, talkin' rings roun' the lot of them.

A stayed at home all over Christmas an' the nixt

march a went te was in the new year. It was a long march that started in Belfast on the first of January an' took four days te get te Derry. A joined it when it got te our town on the third day. At the bottom of our town the polis tried te stap us from gettin' through but there was such a crowd of people in the march that by just standin' tight thegether an' pushin' we managed te break through the cordon. In no time atall we were all headin' up the road in the direction of the nixt town, singin' —

We shall overcome,
We shall overcome,
We shall overcome some day.

Deep in my heart
I do believe,
We shall overcome some day.

Ivery now an' again we passed by housin' estates an' the people come out to look at us. At some estates they would be shoutin' encouragement an' givin' us cups of tay an' mince pies an' pieces of Christmas cake, but at others they would be hurlin' abuse at us an' callin' us effin popish scum. When we walked along chantin', wan man, wan vote, they jeered back at us, wan man, wan woman, because wan of our members was reputed te have a slightly unorthodox sex life. We just waved an' shouted, Seasons Greetin's an' Happy New Year back te them, but they spit at us as we went by.

That night the marchers stapped te rest in a town about ten miles outside Derry. A went home te spen' the night an' rejoined them in the mornin'. There was some great excitement in the crowd that day because ivery body was lookin' forward te arrivin' in Derry in the evenin'. When we set aff, bright an' early, we were singin' —

We're on our way to Derry,
We shall not be moved.
We're on our way to Derry,
We shall not be moved.

Just like a tree that's
Standin' by the water's side
We shall not be moved.

Some time between ten an' eleven a-clock that
mornin' as we were all marchin' along, singin' an'
chantin' in quare form allthegether, a bighead polisman
way a loud hailer an' a blackthorn stick, stapped us
along the road an' toul us that there was a small group
of Paisleyites waitin' ahead at Burntollet Bridge an' he
expected them te throw some stones at us. He said that
the best thing for us te do was te link arms way each
other an' keep movin' forward way our heads down an'
not te panic because hes men had the situation under
control an' they would do iverythin' in their power te
protect us. We all linked arms an' moved forward like
he toul us, singin' away as we did before —

We're on our way to Derry,
We shall not be moved.

Wheniver we landed up at the bridge, it soon
become clear te us all that the big head polisman had
got hes facts wile terrible wrong. The small group of
Paisleyites that he toul us about turned out te be a
wheen of hundred strong. Some of them were wearin'
the helmets an' uniforms of the 'B' specials an' they
were all doin' a war dance an' chantin' as they charged
down the slope at us clutchin' crow bars, an' clubs, an'
coshes, an' cudgels way big rusty six-inch nails stickin'
outa them, an' gaffes, an' bill hooks, an' scythes, an'
picks, an' pitchforks, an' partisans, an' many other kine
of wile dangerous lookin' implements too numerous te
mention.

Up in the field above the road it wasn't just the
Paisleyites that had gathered te greet us, because ivery
wheen of feet, these big high heaps of heavy rock, that
had come from a quarry down the road, were sittin'
stacked up waitin' for us too. The marchers weren't
prepared for anythin' like this size of an attack so a lot

131

of panic broke out when they seen what they were faced way.

Some of them run away back in the direction we had come from, some of them jumped over the ditch on the left han' side that sloped away down te the river, an' some mad mortals like mesel' who really did believe that we could not be moved, stood our groun' on the road for a while an' kept on singin' our song —

We're on our way to Derry,
We shall not be moved.

As soon as the rocks started te. bounce aff us, we collectively come te the hasty conclusion that maybe Derry wasn't the place we were headin' for atall, so some of us started te rise te the occasion by up-datin' the words we were singin' —

We're on our way to heaven.
We shall not be moved.
We're on our way to heaven,
We shall not be moved.
Just like a tree that's
Standin' by the water's side,
We shall not be moved.

Wheniver the Paisleyites heard this song they made it known te us that Derry wasn't the only place where they intended we shouldn't go.

A have always been of the opinion that a body has te die sometime, so when a was hit on the back for the fifth time way a rock that winded me, a fell te the groun' an' lay there way me arms wrapped tight roun' me head, thinkin' that me number was up. A suppose a should of been sayin' me prayers te save me soul from iverlastin' hell, but the only thing a could do at the time was think of me poor ma an' all the trouble she musta went te havin' me, an' hope wile hard that she would be able te get over me tragic death, an' that the memory of it wouldn't blight the whole rest of hir life on hir.

As a was lyin' there thinkin', somebody that called me

a fuckin' Fenian bastard started te kick me an' rain blows down on tap of me way some heavy implement that a could feel but didn't risk lookin' up at, despite me curiosity. Then somebody musta come te save me from me attacker, for a heard another voice, just as the blows stapped, sayin', are ye tryin' te murder hir, ye cowardly bastard ye, can't ye see that she's only a wain? Me attacker set te the man that was tryin' te save me, an' the man that was tryin' te save me said te me in a wile urgent kine of a voice, if ye can manage te stan', get up now for god's sake, for the coast is fairly clear an' get outa here quick.

A didn't risk anythin' so drastic as gettin' up te run, because a can sometimes be a very cautious sort of a person, so instead a just got onte me han's an knees an' crawled inte the ditch on the right han' side of the road, which was the side that the first-class citizens were attackin' from.

Wheniver a got in behine the protection of the hedge, the first thing a done was grope about an' soon a come across another body huddled in there too. It didn't seem te be attackin' anybody so a allowed that it must be wan of us, an' a risked creepin' up wile close te it an' sayin', we mustn't stay in here long, let's get out thegether.

The body then stood up an' lifted me up too way its arm tight roun' me, an' it opened up its coat an' caught my head an' stuck it up inside its jumper. Then it buttoned up its coat again way me inside it. Nixt the body started te edge outa the hedge way its arms still roun' me, an' its back facin' up in the direction of the ambush. The body was a fair bit bigger than me but a could still feel the thud of the rocks vibratin' through me wheniver they hit it on the back.

A don't know how long it took us te get across the bridge but it musta been a quare wee while because we were movin' sideways an' couldn't look where we were goin'. We kept trippin' over boulders an' ivery wheen of would launch a fresh attack te try te finish us aff. Half way across a nearly passed out because a couldn't breathe inside the coat an' jumper, so the body had te loosen its coat at the neck, an' houl down the tap of its jumper te let me get some air.

Wheniver the noise that was goin' on aroun' us sounded at a bit of a distant from the body an' me, we stapped edgin' sideways for a minute an' stood listenin' for a while, an' right enough, we did seem te have come clear of the battle groun'. The body opened up its coat an' a pulled me head outa its jumper an' looked up at its face an' foun' out that the body was a handsome young man way a big bloody gash just above hes right eye. Hes name, appropriately enough, was Armstrong, an' later on that day he introduced me te hes ma, a nice wee worried lookin' woman way a headscarf on hir hair, who had come outa the Bogside te meet the marchers an' look for hir son after she had heard about the ambush on the wireless.

It musta been a miracle, but nobody got killed that day an' soon after we got across the bridge, cars an' ambulances started arrivin' from both directions te help the marchers an' bring the badly injured te hospital.

Wheniver this happened, the first-class citizens run away an' nobody has iver been arrested for takin' part in that ambush te this day, even though the polis knew damned well who the culprits were because they could be seen, laughin' an' chattin' te many of them, on the very best of terms, while the ambush was on.

After our wounds had been cleaned up an' the whole area thoroughly searched te make sure that nobody was left lyin' behine dyin', the wans of us that were still able te walk or limp, set aff again thegether on the road te Derry, singin' a different song, an' wavin' blood-stained hankies above our heads on sticks, at the bit that went

Raise the scarlet flag triumphantly.

We were movin' much slower than before, an' it started

te rain, just as we were comin' close te the Irish Green Estate, near Altnagalvin hospital. The first-class citizens that greeted us there were of a slightly different variety te the wans we had just encountered. They were all too feeble te be travellin' te the bridge at Burntollet, because they were mostly semi-housebound housewives way bad legs an' piles an' some terrible big operations.

They reminded me for all the worl' of the weemen outa 'Korea' the day that they attacked the breadman, only they didn't seem as well organised. They had te resort te pokin' at us way toast forks, an' emptyin' their chamber pots over our heads, so we didn't even bother te bid them the time of day as we passed by.

As soon as we landed in Guildhall Square there was wile commotion. A big crowd of people were waitin' there te welcome us. They shook us by the han's an' asked us wile worried questions about the ambush at Burntollet. Somebody shoved a loud hailer inte me han' an' people started te lift me up on te the back of a lorry te say a few words te the crowd because they thought a was a student on account of the fact that a looked like somebody that had an awful lot te learn.

Wheniver a was on the back of the lorry, me wee brother (the wan that took over me drawer) spotted me an' come over te me runnin', glad te see that a was in wan whole piece. After he was finished quizzin' me about me bruises, an' examinin' me te see that no bits of me were broke or missin' (it runs in the family), he asked me was a hungry, an' a said a was, so he took me te a cafe an' ordered a big feed.

We were sittin' there aten when a gipsy woman way a wee ba wrapped up inside a shawl come inte the cafe an' walked up te the people behine the counter. They toul hir that if she didn't make hirsel' scarce, they would get the polis out te hir. She was headin' back out the door again but me wee brother stapped hir an' toul the people in the cafe that she was te be given whativer she wanted te ate an' he was payin'.

After the three of us had finished aten, the wee gipsy woman called down ivery curse an' plague an' affliction that could be thought of (an' a wheen of others as well) on the owner of the cafe an' all the people that worked there. Then she put the blessin's of almighty god an' hes holy mother, an' all the saints of Ireland, on me an' me wee brother, an' we were surely in need of them too, for we were goin' te the pictures.

Now a suppose a body could be forgive for believin', as a did then, that goin' te the pictures isn't a particularly hazardous activity, but that only goes te show how wrong a body can be. As soon as me an' me wee brother said cheerio te the wee gipsy woman, we walked up the Stran' Road from the cafe back inte Guildhall Square an' then turned right through the arch in the wall te head up in the direction of the ABC cinema.

We had only got about fifty yards from the arch when a crowd of polismen way steel helmets on their heads an' riot shields an' batons in their han's, rushed outa an entry an' blocked our way. Me an' me wee brother stapped. Wan of the polismen toul us te get back through the arch. We toul the polismen that we were goin' te the ABC cinema, an' that the ABC cinema was up in the direction that we were headin'. A polisman called us fuckin' Fenian bastards an' toul us that he would smash our brains out if we didn't turn roun' an' get through the arch. A said te him, that it was a right hearin'-tella allthegether that a body couldn't go te the pictures in Derry without bein' threatened way murder. He lifted up hes baton an' tried te hit me way it but the polisman who was standin' beside him caught hes arm an' said te him, for Christ's sake. A said, thank you te the polisman beside him.

Then a said te all the polismen, will ye's please excuse us, gentlemen, an' let us past, because we want te get te the ABC cinema. The polismen pointed way their batons at the arch an' said, you go that way, dear. A pointed way me finger in the opposite direction an' said te the polismen, now it's clear te me that you nice gentlemen don't know Derry half as well as a do, but please believe me when a tell ye's that the ABC cinema is up that way.

A started te walk in the direction of the ABC cinema an' me wee brother follied me. Two of the polismen grabbed a hoult of me wee brother an' dragged him over te the side, an' said te him, you look like a nice sensible chap, you wouldn't like te see hir gettin' hurt, so why don't ye talk some sense te hir an' get hir te go back through the arch.

Me wee brother said te them, can't ye's just get it in through yer big thick skulls that we are goin' te a picture house that is up that way, an' he pointed te it way hes foot. While me wee brother was talkin', a slipped in between two of the polismen that were blockin' me way an' a started te run up the road in the direction of the picture house. A polisman swung hes baton at me head. A got me arm up just in time te save me skull but the blow slowed me down an' the polisman grabbed a hoult of me an' raised hes baton again.

A turned roun' quick te the polisman an' stuck me head in underneath hes chin. A put me arm (the wan he hadn't hit) tight roun' hes neck. The polisman tried (unsuccessfully) te get me te stap clingin' te him. He had a nice new gleamin' weddin' ring on hes finger, so a said te him, a suppose ye'r goin' te tell yer wife when ye get home from work an' she asks ye what kine of a day ye had, that ye murdered a wee girl of five feet tall be hittin' hir over the head way yer baton, just because she wanted te go te the pictures. De ye imagine that she's goin' te be wile proud of ye when she finds out?

He said, look here, a'm not tryin' te murder anybody. Well, a said te him, in that case Mister, ye could of fooled me. A'm only actin' accordin' te instructions, he said. An' a'm only goin' te the pictures, a said. Ye can't go up that way, he said. A can't get te the picture house any other way, a said. A'm only doin' me duty, he said. At the risk of repeatin' mesel', a said, a'm only goin' te the pictures.

A could see that this conversation was gettin' us nowhere so a let go of hes neck an' shot past him an' run as fast as a could up the road in the direction of the ABC but hes legs were longer than mine an' he soon caught up way me an' started te drag me back in the direction of the arch. Me wee brother, who was still bein' held be two other polismen, could do nothin' but shout at me assailant an' challenge him te a duel out in the middle of a big fiel' somewhere where he would soon show him what he thought of men that beat up weemen.

The polisman didn't try te kill me again after that but he still wouldn't change hes mine an' he started shovin' me way all hes might back down towards the arch, but as he shoved me in wan direction, a kept goin' in the other, all the time sayin' te him, please Mister, a want te go te the pictures, a want te see *Darby O'Gill An' The Little People,* a've been savin' up for weeks, gone an' let me go te the pictures, please, please, a beg ye mister, please, let me go te the pictures.

As soon as the polisman shoved me through the arch inte the arms of the crowd that had gathered te watch from the other side, they all started te hug me an' slap me on me badly bruised back an' tell me how brave a was. The crowd then caught a hoult of the polisman an' started te pull him limb from limb. Wheniver a tried te stap them a nearly got mesel' kilt be me own admirers of a minute before so a went away feelin' sorry for the polisman, because a knew that he was only tryin' te do hes duty be upholdin' the laws that were made for all of us be the acutely deranged, imbecilic, illegitimate, offspring of the mother of parliaments.

They say that bad news travels fast an' a suppose they must be right, because word of my death reached home before a did. When a landed in the back door late that night way me wee brother, a foun' me da sittin' mournin' at the tap of the table way hes head restin' in hes han's, an' me ma rushin' aroun' at breakneck speed, tryin' te make the house all ready for the wake.

Wheniver the two of them got over the shock of seein' the dead alive, they put me inte bed an' a wasn't able te move outa it for a long time because ivery part of me was black an' blue an' bleedin' an' swollen. For the nixt wheen of days all the neighbours kept comin' in te examine me, an' commend me ma for havin' such a brave daughter, because a was wan of only about half a dozen girls that had made it across the Burntollet bridge.

A stayed in me bed for a wheen of weeks an' wheniver a got up a started te prepare mesel' for the future be practisin' some basic skills that a thought might come in useful if iver a went out te look for work again like, combin' me hair, movin' me head from side te side slowly, an' noddin' it up an' down a bit, sittin' down an' risin' up from a chair without bein' helped, puttin' on me own clothes, tyin' me shoes, walkin'. After a was satisfied that a'd acquired sufficient skills, a set out again in search of work, but a decided not te go back te Belfast, as it was clear for all te see that me an' Belfast weren't made for each other so a allowed that a would give Dublin a try instead.

Chapter 8

Me first impression of Dublin
was that it was big an' if ye weren't very careful ye could
get lost in it. Me wee brother had gone te Dublin a
wheen of weeks before me on account of the fact that it
was aisier te get te the pictures there than it was in
Derry, so when a landed in Dublin a had hes address but
a didn't know how te get te it. As luck would have it
though, a had a tongue in me cheek so a decided te ask
somebody for directions. The oul wan that a quizzed toul
me te take a number nineteen bus all the way te the
terminus. As soon as a thanked hir a seen a nineteen bus
comin' an' a got on it.

While a was gettin' aff at the other en' a asked the
conductor could he direct me te me brother's digs an'
when a give him the address he toul me it was fifteen
miles away. A toul him that an oul wan had toul me te
take a number nineteen bus te the terminus an' that that
was what a had done. He toul me that a had got the
right bus, only it was goin' in the wrong direction. A
asked him what the hell the number nineteen bus was
doin', goin' in the wrong direction. He started te roar an'
laugh at me an' he said te the driver, we've got a right
culchie here, Mick. A toul him what he could do way
hes number nineteen bus an' got aff.

Me second impression of Dublin was that it was even bigger than a had at first imagined, an' that even if ye were very careful, ye could still get lost in it. A was dead beat four hours later when a finally arrived at me wee brother's digs. Hes lan'lady was nice so she took me in an' give me a big feed an' toul me about the quare nice sort of a fella that me brother was, an' a agreed.

Wheniver me brother got home from hes work he bought an evenin' paper, then him an' me an' a fella called John from our town, who lived in the same digs, went out an' got on a bus te go inte town te look for a place for me te stay. There were lots of flats for girls in the paper, but we didn't bother te search for any that night. We contented oursel's instead be lookin' for a bed an' breakfast place for me te stay in for a wheen of days till a was sorted out way a job.

We tried two or three bed an' breakfast places in the city centre before we foun' wan that suited. At the first place we came te, me wee brother didn't like the look of some of the people who were hangin' aroun'.

At the second place, the people didn't think a lot of the look of us. It was after nine a-clock at night when we come te a place that suited iverybody, that is if a was agreed te share a room way another girl for the night. A said a would.

Me wee brother said, not so fast, our Ann, what de ye know about this girl that ye'r agreein' te share a room way, she could be anybody for all you know. He toul the woman that owned the boardin' house that he would like te have a few words way the girl in the room before he left hes sister way hir. The woman said she was in number fifteen, so the three of us headed up the stairs. As soon as me brother knocked on the door, a girl's voice called, come in, an' so he opened the door an' walked straight inte the room. A follied in after him, an' John, who was wan of the most inoffensive souls that iver walked the face of this

141

earth, but didn't look it, stood in the frame of the door. It was only six feet high, an' John was six feet six. He had jet black crazed lookin' crooked eyes, an' a huge nose that veered dangerously te wan side half way down, an' tried unsuccessfully te rectify itsel' be swingin' back hopelessly in the other direction. He bent hes knees out towards the doorposts te make himsel' fit more comfortably in the doorframe while me wee brother carried on way hes business.

The girl, who was in hir late twenties, was sittin' up in bed readin' a Mills an' Boon romance, called *Passion Beneath the Palms*. Me brother said te hir, wile polite, excuse us Miss, for walkin' in on ye an' you in yer bed, but this here is my sister who's thinkin' about stayin' the night here, so a just want te check te see if the place is safe.

Me wee brother went over te the window an' looked te see if it was securely locked, an' after he was satisfied, he asked the girl did she sleep with the window open, an' she said she didn't. Then me wee brother went te check the door an' he asked John te stan' outa hes way till he could close it an' try the lock. John come an' stood in the middle of the room, an' the girl in the bed looked up at him, an' the book she was readin' was shakin' in hir han' like a leaf.

Wheniver me wee brother was fully satisfied that the room was safe enough, he allowed that a could stay there for a night or two till a got mesel' fixed up way a job an' a flat. He warned me an' the girl in the bed te keep the door an' the window locked at all times, because Dublin was no safe place for weemen te live in on their own. Me an' me wee brother an' John went downstairs then, an' me wee brother toul the lan'lady that the room seemed all right te him, but he would appreciate it a lot if she would lock up the front door as soon as he left because ye niver know what kine of rare characters might just walk in aff the street, an' it was highly unlikely that she would get any more customers at that time of the night.

A went back up te the room as soon as they were gone, an' a said te the girl in the bed that a was sorry about me brother. She said not te apologise for she only wished she had a brother that cared as much about hir. But whether she meant that or not is a different matter entirely. A learned from the lan'lady that she had come over from Galway te see about gettin' a visa te work in America but she'd been havin' second thoughts about emigratin'. Nivertheless, three days later she flew outa Ireland te go te the States, niver te return.

For the next wheen of days a spent most of me time phonin' up about jobs an' flats. It wasn't long before a got fixed up way a job, an' although a didn't get a flat te go way it, a foun' what a thought was the nixt best thing, digs, in a nice quiet suburb, right beside the hospital where a was te work as an assistant nurse.

Me lan'lady was a woman in hir middle forties who was married te a merchant seaman that come home on visits te hir, two times a year. At eight a-clock ivery mornin' from Monday till Friday, she drove inte the city te hir work in a factory that made weemen's overalls an' aprons. After work each day she brought home a boxful of sewin' te keep hirsel' busy throughout the evenin'. All hir neighbours believed that she was a secretary in the factory office, an' she made the three people that rented hir rooms swear niver te disclose te anybody outside the four walls of hir house that she was only a machinist, because it would mean hir havin' te sell up an' lave the area in disgrace.

Wheniver a rang up about the room she accepted me way open arms because she thought a was a qualified nurse. After she foun' out that a wasn't she soon made it known te me that she didn't usually cater for people from the lower orders. She toul me that the neighbours all thought a was qualified an' if a iver let it slip that a wasn't, she would ask me te lave without notice. A assured hir that a would try me hardest te pass mesel' aff as a member of the gentry by follyin' hir high example.

The hospital where a got the job was only newly opened an' it had three wings named after St Brigid, St Patrick, an' St Columkill, the three national saints of Ireland. It was a private hospital run be nuns for mentally handicapped wains way rich parents. The chief nurse there was a nun called Sister Boniface, an' she made the wains do what they were toul by beatin' them over their heads way a wooden spoon.

When the rich parents come te visit their wains on a Sunday afternoon, Sister Boniface would walk about way them through the wards, tellin' them about their wains' progress in the friendliest possible way. She even admitted that she maintained discipline be showin' the wains the wooden spoon. Needless te say, she would add, smilin', one would niver consider usin' it, an' the poor rich parents believed hir.

Before a was workin' in the hospital for long, a got mesel' two pet patients. Wan was a wee girl of five called Mary. After a started workin' there she wouldn't let any of the other nurses near hir. She was so beautiful that a could have spent the rest of me life just sittin' lookin' at hir. Mary was supposed te be a deaf mute. Wan day when a had been workin' there for about a fortnight, there was a nice fresh shower of snow, so me an' two of the nurses took a wheen of the wains out te play in it. A was lookin' at Mary as a robin that was hoppin' about in the snow behine hir chirped an' hir eyes darted in the direction that the sound came from. A come te the conclusion that Mary was about as deaf as a was, so a started te tell the staff about it. Ivery nurse on the entire St Columkill wing, which was the wing that Mary lived in, dismissed me theory so completely as te refuse even te discuss it.

A decided not te let the matter rest so a made an appointment te see wan of the people who had interviewed me for the job, a woman psychologist from Austria. Wheniver she heard about Mary's eyes an' the robin, she was greatly interested an' give instructions te the nursin' staff that Mary was te be more closely observed.

The nurses on the wing were not very pleased way me for darin' te go above their heads, so they assumed an attitude of haughty superiority an' made it known te me that my function was te wash, dress, an' feed the patients, an' lave matters of a higher nature up te them, the qualified, who had studied for years, an' could now take pulses an' temperatures, an' give injections, an' fill in patients' progress cards.

As soon as a guessed that Mary wasn't deaf, a took te talkin' te hir more, an' askin' hir what she thought of things, in the way a would talk te any wain. Ivery night a toul hir a different fairy tale like 'Hansel and Gretal', 'Snow White and the Seven Dwarfs', 'Little Red Riding Hood'. Wan night when a had finished tellin' the story of 'Goldilocks and the Three Bears' te Mary, a tucked hir up in bed an' was about te lave the ward when a heard a wee voice sayin', 'sore'. A turned back an' foun' that she was pointin' te hir stomach that had been covered for a year or more way a festerin' sore that niver improved because no one could find a way te stap hir from pickin' at it. A give hir a cuddle an' toul hir te go te sleep because it was late, but a didn't let on that a noticed anythin' strange about hir speakin'.

A couldn't sleep that night way the excitement of havin' proof that Mary wasn't deaf or dumb, so a landed at the hospital early nixt mornin' te tell the chief nurse about it. The chief nurse brought me down te Mary's ward an' she started te quiz Mary about what she said the night before te me. Mary didn't answer. The chief nurse wasn't surprised. That night when a put Mary te bed, the same thing happened, an' as luck would have it, nobody else was about.

It was nearly a week later that a managed te convince the rest of the staff that Mary could talk, be gettin' wan of them te hide in behine a curtain when a was puttin' hir te bed.

Me other pet patient was a wee boy of seven called Leonard. He got thumped over the head way the wooden spoon more often than the others because he was violent. Leonard was the eldest wain in a family of ten an' he took five epileptic fits ivery day. He had no time atall for other people, an' if iver wan of them got near enough te him, it always ended up way a black eye or a bloody nose.

Ivery time Leonard attacked me, a held him out at arms length an' joked an' laughed way him, tellin' him te quit hes oul tomfoolery or a would set me ma on te him, an' hir a terrible oul witch of a woman that could niver stan' no nonsense from nobody. A soon begin te notice that Leonard only attacked people because he expected them te attack him, but if he foun' out that people meant him no harm, he could be placid enough.

After me success way Mary a decided te spen' more time way Leonard as none of the other staff paid him much attention because of hes violence. He was kept under control way drugs an' a daily hammerin' from the wooden spoon. Wan day when a had been workin' there for about four months a decided that a didn't want te stan' aroun' doin' nothin' for Leonard any longer so a asked for an appointment way Sister Boniface te talk about him.

She made it clear te me at the onset of our confab that she didn't have any time for sittin' roun' talkin', so a toul hir right away that a thought Leonard wasn't a violent wain atall as he only seemed te attack people when he thought they were tryin' te hurt him. She toul me that she'd niver heard such a preposterous suggestion in all of hir life, an' that a would do well te go away an' think about me whole attitude towards me

146

position at the hospital. Then she set down at hir desk an' started te go about hir ordinary business as if a wasn't there.

Nixt day at dinner time wheniver Sister Boniface started te discipline Leonard way the wooden spoon for throwin' hes dinner on the floor an' tryin' te scratch the eyes outa the nurse who was houlin' him down an' prizin' hes mouth open for another wan te feed him, a grabbed the wooden spoon from hir an' set it at an angle between the wall an' the floor an' smashed it te pieces way me heel.

After dinner, as requested, a reported te the office where Sister Boniface give me a lecture an' the sack. In hir lecture, she toul me that she was in charge of the spiritual an' pastoral well bein' of all the patients an' staff that god had seen fit te place in hir care. She assured me that she found it as painful te have te sack an unsuitable member of staff as she did te have te control a violent patient, like Leonard.

A toul hir that Leonard wasn't a violent patient, but an innocent wain, imitatin' the behaviour of people like hir, who taught him violence. She toul me te lave hir office at once. A said a would go if she explained te me why this dangerous violent boy had stapped showin' any signs of aggression towards me.

She started talkin' all kines of oul shit about hir painful duty, an' Christ bein' hir witness, so a toul hir that a had niver come across any evidence in Christ's teachin' te support hir view that it was laudable an' right an' proper te beat wains over the heads way wooden spoons, an' a suggested that now that she didn't have a wooden spoon, she might like te try, just for wance, te do things different. She opened up hir drawer an' proudly took out a whole big pile of wooden spoons that had the name of the hospital carved on their handles te let me see the kine of a gullible peasant a was for believin' that anythin' a could do would make any difference te hir.

A lost me temper at that an' toul hir what a thought about people like hir who weren't just satisfied abusin' helpless wains, but had te go so far as te try te make out that te do so was some kine of a fuckin' virtue. A toul hir if she cared a damn about the patients in hir care, the first thing she would realise was that the patients were all wains, an' that wains are not so much in our care as at our mercy. An' if we don't treat wains right, there is nothin' they can do, because wains have no unions. They canny get back at us if we abuse them. An' wains that canny talk are even more at our mercy than wains that can, because they're not even able te complain. So people like hir have a free choice way wains that canny talk. They can treat them way the respect that they deserve, or they can beat them up way wooden spoons an' nobody will be anythin' the wiser. They can even quote Christ te reinforce their arguments in favour of abuse, but they needn't come that fuckin' crap way me, because a can quote them Christ for Christ until the cows come home, an' a can tell them Christ was niver in favour of abusin' poor wee helpless wains. A toul hir too, that a wanted hir to know wance an' for all what a lot of other people thought an' didn't have the nerve te say — that she was a bully an' a coward for beatin' up wains that didn't have any way of gettin' back at hir — that wains had feelin's — that wains had rights — that wains deserve the same consideration as anybody else — even wains that couldn't talk — that wains are PEOPLE too. Then a picked up the telephone an' flung it at hir head, for the sight of hir, cowerin' in the corner way a face on hir like a frightened ferret made me want te puke.

After that a got mesel' a job in an undertakers makin' shrouds, but a had te move outa me digs because the lan'lady couldn't stan' the disgrace of having somebody that got sacked be a nun livin' in hir house. A was lucky though, because the first time a

148

looked in a paper a saw an advertisement for a flat te be let out te a respectable, young, Irish, catholic business-lady way good references, just aroun' the corner from the morgue.

A picked out three of me references (wan from the parish priest way the cure that used te rub me all over way hes han's an' ask me all kines of questions about chastity, sayin' that a was a great paragon of virtue an' innocence allthegether an' that he would have no hesitation atall in recommendin' me for any post or for adoption inte any family lucky enough te have me; wan from the headmaster of the school that didn't want te have anythin' te do way our family in the first place, sayin' that he had known me parents for many years an' they were industrious, respectable, an' good Christians, an' sayin' nothin' atall about me on account of the fact that he didn't know me; an' wan from Frank sayin' that a was lovely an' good an' intelligent an' funny, an' that he expected me to go wile far – presumably as far as possible away from him, which a have), an' a headed aff te meet the lan'lady.

The very second that a rang the bell the door was opened an' a deep tenor voice from the hallway said, step right this way, young lady. Me eyes took a wheen of seconds te adjust te the different light an' then a seen the lan'lady. In all me born days a had niver seen anybody that looked remotely like hir, an' a couldn't quite make up me mine whether she was a man or a woman. She stood six feet three inches tall an' had very broad shoulders. She wore a hat that looked like a flower pot turned upside down an' although she was well past middle age hir hair was yellow like corn an' it stuck out from in under the hat like the strands of an unfanked rope.

Me first reaction was te laugh an' then te run away but a was kinda desperate for a place te stay so a stepped inside as a was bid. In the hall a seen another wee woman of about sixty-five or so standin' way a wee smile on hir face, lookin' uncomfortably at me, so a smiled back at hir. The lan'lady closed the door behine me an' spoke sharply te the other wee woman. Where's yer manners, she said, don't keep the young lady waitin' in the lobby, show hir inte the parlour.

As soon as we got inte the parlour the big wan toul me that the first thing she needed te do was check me references, because if they were not satisfactory, that would be the en' of the matter as she made a point of only rentin' hir apartments out te the most highly recommended, superior, respectable, good-livin', young, Irish catholic business-ladies.

Wheniver she had finished readin' all me references three times, an' houlin' them up te the light te look through them, for reasons known only te hirsel' an' maybe god, she stuck out hir han' an' caught a hoult of mine an' give it a hearty shake. Ma name is Miss McBride, an' this here is ma sister Mary, she said. A have recently returned to Dublin from the U.S. of A. where a'd been a teacher for over twenty years, yes-sir-ee. A have bought up several properties in this area with the intention of providin' apartments for respectable, young, Irish catholic business-ladies like yourself Miss Glone. A have been aroun' an' a know how hard it can be sometimes be te keep up standards when yer far away from home, so a believe that a have somethin' really positive te contribute. That's what a'm here for, Miss Glone, te help an' guide at any time. So just make yourself at home here, a will think that a have failed if you don't make yourself right at home. A assured hir that a had started te feel at home the very minute a stepped over hir threshold.

Miss McBride lived in a house way hir timid wee sister, just aroun' the corner from the flat. She took hir duty very serious indeed, an' had a habit of lettin' hirsel' in unannounced at ivery hour of the day an' night te check up on the behaviour of hir highly recommended, superior, respectable, good-livin', young, Irish catholic business-ladies.

The flat a had was on the first floor, an' two girls from Sligo, wan a civil servant, the other a nurse, lived on the floor underneath. They were both engaged te be married, an' wan mornin' at six a-clock Miss McBride walked straight inte their bedrooms an' foun', much te hir horror, the two of them sleepin' way their boyfrien's. The hullabaloo that followed woke the whole house up so a went downstairs te see what was wrong. A foun' Miss McBride hurlin' all the girls belongings out inte the middle of the street, an' screamin' te passers-by te look at the hookers, hookers, that were livin' right underneath hir roof. The two girls an' their boyfrien's were standin' lookin' on, shocked, an' terrified, an' starkers.

After Miss McBride had finished evictin' the hookers, she landed up the stairs te me an' hir tremblin' from head te toe an' nearly in tears. A tried te get hir te sit down but she wasn't te be comforted. She toul me how she had foun' a box of the most terrible contraptions, that were banned by the church an' the state, sittin' down in a drawer in hir very own house, an' how she had te touch these contraptions way hir own han's, an' how if she niver did anythin' else but wash an' scrub for the rest of hir life she couldn't get hir han's clean again.

At the time she landed up way me a was halfway through me breakfast — eight ginger snap biscuits an' a pint of guinness. Wheniver she begin te get hir senses back an' take notice she said, now what is that that you're drinkin' there, Miss Glone? A said, forgive me bad manners for not offerin' ye a sup, it's a pint of the guinness a'm drinkin'. A would not wish you to offer me any of that, Miss Glone, she said, for a do not approve of alcoholic beverages.

Well, a said, Miss Bride, that makes two of us, for a don't approve of alcoholic beverages either an' if ye ask me anythin', a'd say that alcoholic beverages is the

151

curse of the Irish. But tell me Miss Bride, whereiver did ye get the notion that guinness was an alcoholic beverage when iverybody knows that it's so fortified way vitimins an' minerals that it's nothin' more than liquid cornflakes?

Now tell me this, Miss Bride, a said, changin' the subject fast, how was it that these two hookers managed te get inte yer house, was it way faked references that they conned ye? Well, she said, Miss Glone, that's a very good question, but a'm not that easily taken in. Life has taught me niver te judge anythin' at its face value. When a'm shown references, a always contact the people that wrote them, just to make double-sure. The parish priest that a phoned up in Sligo told me that these two girls were flawless, Miss Glone.

Then, a said, in that case, Miss Bride, what de ye think happened te the two of them in the meantime te turn them inte such vile hookers? How did they come te fall from grace so quick? It's an easy enough thing te fall from grace, she said, an' it's because a know that so well that a took over these apartments te be of some help an' guidance te poor lonely catholic girls, far away from home, Miss Glone.

Why did ye fail way these two, Miss Bride? a asked. A didn't fail way them, Miss Glone, she assured me, it was them that failed way me. They were not, you must under-stand, young ladies like yourself, Miss Glone. The pair of them were haughty an' stand-offish from the very beginnin'. They made it clear to me that a had no right to be interferin' in their lives — an' them livin' in ma very own house. A said, ye don't say, Miss Bride, does that not go te show that some people have no respect atall?

The crack was gettin' far too good te lave then, so a decided not te go te me work that day an' a poured mesel' out another wee glass of guinness. Tell me, Miss Bride, a said, what kine of things were these contraptions that ye foun' in the box in the drawer? Could ye describe them te me so as a'll know what they look like an' niver be unfortunate enough to touch them way me han's like you did, for ye see, me ma was not like you, Miss Bride, she niver taught me anythin' about the ways of the worl' an' a'm feared livin' here on me own in this big city full of all kines of terrible things an' sinful contraptions that a know nothin' about.

Now, Miss Glone, said Miss McBride, there are some people, an' good people too, your dear mother would appear to be wan of them, who honestly believe that ignorance is bliss. A do not happen te belong te that particular school of thought, so a will try ma best to answer any questions that you care to ask me, as openly an' as honestly as possible. A'll begin' by tellin' you about these contraptions that we've spoken about. They are made from rubber an' used to prevent conception, and, not meanin' any offence to your good self, Miss Glone, they come outa the north of Ireland.

God almighty protect us all this good holy day, a said, but how does these terrible contraptions manage te prevent conception? Does these vile hooker weemen stick them up inte their wombs or what? These contraptions are used by men, not weemen, my dear Miss Glone, Miss McBride said te me. Well, a said to hir, get along way ye, a niver. Even a know that men canny conceive wains, only weemen can.

Dear me, said Miss McBride, a fear a haven't explained myself well, so a'll start from the very beginnin'. When sexual intercourse takes place, the male organ is placed inside the female organ where it plants its seeds an' that is how the woman comes te conceive. That must take a bit of doin', a said, a thing like that. How is it that the male organ doesn't just slither out before it has time te be plantin' any seeds? Male organs look like slippery wee things te me, Miss Bride.

They become erect dear, before bein' placed inside the female. But tell me, Miss Glone, she said, changin' the subject suspiciously, how have you managed to learn so much about the appearance of male organs? Well, a said, Miss Bride, in the past a have seen a quare wheen of them when a was changin' wee wains nappies, an' a have spotted a couple more recently — just downstairs this mornin'.

But ye tell me that they become erect, an' that's a mystery te me, how de ye mean, erect, Miss Bride? a persisted. By erect, a simply mean hard, Miss Glone, stiff — rigid — firm. A come on now, Miss Bride, a said, what kine of a blitherin' archeegit de ye take me for? De ye expect me te fall for a yarn like that — male organs that become stiff, firm, rigid, an' erect, what in the name of god could be the cause of such a rare thing as that, Miss Bride?

In a word, Miss Glone, lust — lust an' the promptin's of the divil. Ye mean wan of them seven deadly sins, Miss Bride? Indeed a DO, Miss Glone. But tell me, a said, Miss Bride, after this lust attacks these male organs, are they finished aff for good, de these poor sinners have te go about way their organs stiff, rigid, firm, an' erect for the rest of their lives? No, she said, they go back to normal after a while an' stay that way till the divil starts te prompt them again.

A suppose, a said, a lot of them don't have te, for a imagine that when they're stiff, firm, rigid, an' erect like that, they must be very brittle an' easy te break aff. Unfortunately, Miss Glone, said Miss McBride, sadly, that is not the case, they are anythin' but brittle. But they must be brittle, Miss Bride, a insisted, an' surely very long an' thin as well if they have te be goin' up inte the female womb te be plantin' seeds.

You've got it all wrong, corrected Miss McBride. These organs are not thin, Miss Glone, a agree they are long, but not in the least bit thin. God, a said, Miss Bride, are you tellin' me that this lust is such a powerful thing that it has the strength te make male organs become stiff, firm, rigid, an' erect, an' long an' fat as well? That is so, Miss Glone, that is so, repeated Miss McBride, sadly.

Well, a said, a will be damned if a iver heard the like of that, but tell me Miss Bride, what kine of a length would these organs grow te, as long as me finger, would ye say? Much, much, longer, dear. Would they be as thick as me finger then, would ye tell me, Miss Bride? Much, much, thicker. Then would they be the length an' thickness of that, a said, houlin' up me guinness bottle for hir inspection. Yes, she said, studyin' it carefully, they would be more that size, that is closer to the mark.

Now it's a strange worl' we're livin' in an' that's for sure, a said, but tell me wan more thing, Miss Bride, was it in the college where ye trained te be a teacher that ye foun' out about all these awful things? Do poor teachers have te learn all about the sinfulness of the worl' before they are let inte the schools te teach, in the same way that priests have te learn all the terrible doctrines of communism in order te be better at combatin' them, before they're allowed te go out te the missions te preach the word of god te the poor, the sick, an' the needy?

Well, Miss Glone, said Miss McBride, it may come as a great surprise for you te learn this, but a didn't go te college te learn te be a teacher. When a first went out to the U.S. of A. a was a real greenhorn, just like yourself, and like you too, Miss Glone, a was a mighty fine worker. Every mornin', come rain, hail, or shine, a got up early an' went out te business. A'm a great believer in self improvement, Miss Glone, so a didn't just sit aroun' on ma butt. When a was twenty-five years old, a decided that a wanted te become a teacher, an' when a make up ma mind te do somethin', a just go right out there an' do it, so a become an apprentice teacher, yes-sir-ee. After two years, ma apprenticeship was finished, an' then a had a class of ma very own, Ogees-yea, did a have a class of ma own?

Ye sure do surprise me be tellin' me that, Miss Bride, a said, because anybody talkin' te ye would niver suspect for a moment that you didn't have wan of the highest of them there university educations. Now tell me then, Miss Bride, a said, de ye think that if a went out te the U.S. of A. a might get mesel' apprenticed te a teacher too, because te tell ye nothin' but the truth, a said confidentially as a refilled me glass, a've always had a hankerin' like yersel' for self improvement an' a think that a too might make a mighty fine teacher.

It's not as easy gettin' on in the United States today as it was in ma day, Miss Glone, she said, they have started goin' in for all these college graduates they call them, a lot of young upstarts, if ye ask me. In fact, Miss Glone, they have even put negroids into the classrooms. Holy Christ almighty, a said, don't tell me they expected you te teach black wains, Miss Bride. Much worse than that, a can assure ye, she said, they have now got niggers teachin' in schools right alongside the rest of us. It's not decent, Miss Glone, it's not decent. Why, a remember when a first went out te America, niggers knew their place. They stood up an' gave white folk their seats when they got on a bus. They weren't allowed to send their kids to a white school and they didn't have the vote.

Now they're all over the place, callin' themsel's doctors an' nurses an' teachers. Believe it or not, a went te mass one day in downtown Philadelphia, an' there was a nigger, standin' up at the altar sayin' mass, SAYIN' MASS. A'll niver forget it for the rest of ma life, Miss Glone, it isn't right, it isn't decent. A would still be teachin' in that school that a helped te build up, Miss Glone, if they hadn't gone an' put a nigger over me. They expected me te take ma orders from a nigger. The U.S. of A. is a changed place, Miss

Glone, so a wouldn't advise one of ma young ladies te go there atall.

Me an' Miss McBride spent the whole of that mornin' an' most of the afternoon sittin' there confabbin' away, about god, an' sex, an' sin, an' education, an' how travel broadens the mine, an' race, an' politics, an' duty, an' responsibility, an' all the other burnin' issues of the day that interested hir greatly. A niver felt the time movin' by atall, because Miss McBride was easily the most grotesquely fascinatin' individual a had iver come across in the whole of me life.

In all the time that we talked thegether the least hint of a smile niver touched hir face. She had a deadly grey pallor which musta bothered hir a bit because she painted two crude blobs in the middle of hir cheeks an' black shaky lines roun' the outlines of hir eyes. She didn't have any lips, so she made up for their absence by smearin' some shockin' pink paint all aroun' the hole that was sittin' at the bottom of hir nose. It was probably just as well that she didn't try te smile, because only god alone could tell what amount of damage a smile might do te a face like hirs. A have niver quite been able to decide whether she was real, or just some poor character that managed te escape out of wan of Samuel Beckett's plays, te haunt Dublin.

When a was livin' in that flat for a wheen of months, a was walkin' through O'Connell Street wan day when a spotted a fellow of about me own age, from our town, walkin' up the street in my direction, lookin' wile unsteady on hes feet. The first thought that occurred te me was that he was drunk, on account of the fact that it was not entirely unheard of for people from our town te go completely te the bad wheniver they landed in Dublin. (Indeed me ma had already predicted that Dublin would prove to be the ruination of me, an' a'm not sure that she wasn't right.)

As the two of us come up alongside wan another we stapped te have a chat in the way that country people do. A said te him, how are ye doin', sir? Te tell ye the truth, Ann, he said, a'm not doin' very well. Then he toul me how he had nowhere to live, or no job, or money, since hes girlfrien', who's father he had worked for, threw him outa their flat an' wouldn't let him in again te collect hes cards an' wee bits of clothes.

That's a terrible herintella, sir, a said, when did ye last ate? A foun' out that he hadn't tasted a bite of food for nearly a week so a said te him, now this state of affairs can't be allowed te continue, come on home way me this minute till a get ye a feed. A, he said, Ann, it's very good of ye, but a couldn't be doin' that, it's enough ye have te be doin' lookin' after yersel' without botherin' about the likes of me, sure a'm finished.

A said, don't talk such rot, ye'r not finished yet, but if ye carry on much longer the way ye are, ye soon will be, for it's a well-known scientifically proven fact, that if ye don't ate, ye don't shit, an' if ye don't shit, ye die, so come on home way me this minute. As soon as a got him home, a gave him a good feed of gingersnaps an' guinness, an' made him a nice hot bath, an' took hes clothes te the launderette te wash them so that he would look decent wheniver he went searchin' for a job. A toul him that he could sleep on the floor in me kitchen for a wheen of nights till he got himsel' properly thegether again, niver suspectin' for a second that the bold lad had niver had himsel thegether before in the whole of hes life.

At three a-clock that mornin' a was woke up from me sleep way a wile persistant proddin' at me ribs. Wheniver a opened me eyes an seen Miss McBride stooped over me, a allowed that a knew what was comin' nixt, for in the previous week, she had evicted no fewer than eight hookers from the two houses on either side of the wan a lived in.

Miss Glone, she said, in a hoarse whisper, please don't be alarmed, but you better rise an' get dressed at once, there is an intruder in your apartment. A jumped straight outa bed an' then a realised who she was talkin' about so a set down again an' said, Miss Bride, a think you are mistaken, the person you take for an intruder is ma guest. Miss Glone, she said, you surprise me, that exceedingly coarse and unkempt young man your guest?

A said, Miss Bride, now don't you go lettin' yersel' be fooled be appearances, he might look coarse an' unkempt te you but that only goes te prove how misleadin' appearances can sometimes be. A suppose a should let ye inte hes secret, a said, but not before ye promise niver te breathe it te another livin' soul (she promised) for if hes cover was iver blew he couldn't carry on way hes wile important work for god. Ye see, Miss Bride, a said (lowerin' me voice te make sure that a didn't hear what a was sayin' in case a made mesel' laugh), he's a priest workin' in disguise as a down-an'-out te try te fine out if he can, who it is that's behine this recent wave of vice that's been turnin' all these highly-recommended, superior, respectable, good-livin', young, Irish catholic business-ladies inte vile hookers overnight. The church authorities is convinced that it is somebody livin' aroun' this area that is responsible, but if a whiff of this conversation gets out, the whole operation will be scuttled.

After the priest was stayin' in my flat for a wheen of weeks an' showin' no signs of shiftin', a met him wan evenin' when a was comin' outa me work an' he had another fellow of about our age way him who looked even more dejected than the priest himsel'. He said te me, Ann, this here is Charlie McTaggart from Donegal — he's a wee bit down on hes luck an' has nowhere te stay, de ye think ye could put him up for a wheen of days till he gets himsel' straightened out?

A looked this Charlie McTaggart up an' down for a while an' it was clear te me when a was finished that he was indeed down on hes luck, but apart from that he seemed harmless enough, so a took him home an' give him a feed of gingersnaps an' guinness. A didn't bother way the bath or takin' hes clothes te the launderette for a allowed that that might just prove te be another complete waste of time.

Over the nixt wheen of weeks, word about my hospitality spread rapidly roun' certain elements of Dublin society, an' soon the house a lived in was full te the brim way young fellows from ivery part of Ireland, who were down on their luck an' a was the only highly recommended, superior, respectable, good-livin', young, Irish catholic business-lady that would be seen dead within a mile of any of Miss McBride's properties.

Te begin way, Miss McBride had been a wee bit sceptical of me an' the priest, an' had continued te carry out spot checks on the two of us in the middle of the night, for it was quite clear te see that she had niver come across my particular brand of catholic respectability before in hir life an' she wasn't quite sure what te make of it. When the house that a lived in begin te overflow an' fill up the houses on either side that had been cleared of vile hookers by Miss McBride, a decided that it was high time for me te play me trump card, so a toul Miss McBride that a was really a nun, workin' undercover way the priest, an' that we had both been sent te the slums of Dublin te live an' work among young catholic men who were in danger of bein' sucked down inte sin.

When a mentioned the word slum, she was deeply offended an' tried te protest at the slur on hir property, but a just showed hir a photograph of me in me holy habit, shakin' han's way a well known Irish bishop, an' a toul hir that if the place hadn't been a terrible slum in the first place, the church would niver have consigned me te it.

A went on te tell Miss McBride that the church sure did appreciate the work she had started in givin' solace an' comfort te so many young girls who were lonely an' far away from home an' that she had ivery reason te be proud of hirsel' for the standards she had set because if it hadn't been for the very height of hir standards, me an' the priest would have had a great deal of difficulty findin' a suitable base for our missionary activities on account of the fact that not many slum lan'ladies would dream of exercisin' such strict controls over the lives of their lodgers.

A sure did everythin' in ma power te help ma girls, Miss Glone-sister, she said, because a know how hard it can sometimes be te keep up standards when ye'r far away from home. A believe that a really did have somethin' positive to contribute to ma girls. A just wanted to be here to help an' guide them at any time, to make them feel right at home, sister.

After that a toul Miss McBride that me an' hir were clearly two of a kine because it was plain for all the worl' te see that she took the same kine of interest in young ladies that a took in young men an' that we would therefore be able te work well thegether, an' she agreed.

Ma boys an' me got along well most of the time, an' they were all very fond of me. The only trouble was that there were far too many of them for me te keep under proper control, so they often went out foragin' through the town on shopliftin' sprees te get wee presents for me. A just couldn't manage te keep them right atall. But havin' ma boys about did have its compensations, for if iver a felt like goin' for walks aroun' the town in the middle of the night, fifteen or twenty of ma boys would come along too, just te make sure that a got back safe, an' that nobody iver bothered me.

Wan of the many things that ma boys weren't any

good at doin' was washin' their smelly socks, an' so a day come when a just couldn't stick the hoage any longer so a packed me bags an' left them all te the tender care of dear Miss McBride, who became the sad bewildered owner of a row of very dilapidated doss-houses in the middle of Dublin town.

A decided then that what a needed most was a complete change of scene so a gave up me job makin' shrouds an' went to work at a delicatessen, where people that had nothin' better te do way their money could afford te buy their food pre-chewed. A got mesel' digs again instead of a flat because meals were provided at digs, for a allowed that what a needed most was somebody te tell me when te ate, as aten had niver been a particular hobby of mine.

Me new lan'lady had seven wains an' a semi-invalid husband who worked part time as an electrician. All nine members of the family slept in the kitchen of the house, an' ivery night before they went te bed they had te let the fire die an' clean out the fire place te make space for the lan'lady's husband te stretch hes feet.

The three bedrooms in their house was let out te lodgers for three poun' ten shillin's a week, includin' three meals a day. The lan'lady loved te escape from hir kitchen an' come up stairs an' chat te hir lodgers. Ivery time she called in on me the subject of conversation turned te hir life's ambition te visit Rome te see the Holy Father, an' all the art galleries an' the Sistine Chapel roof.

Wan day when a had been livin' there for about three months, a met some girls on me way home from work who had been evicted by Miss McBride. They were goin' te an anti-war demonstration at the American Embassy an' a decided te join them. Two hours later a was outside the embassy, peacefully protestin' way a placard that read, 'Yankee Pigs Get Out Of Vietnam' when a got mesel' arrested.

It wasn't so much an' arrest as a slaughter. Kill the bastards first, an' then arrest them, seemed te have been the attitude of the polis. The guardian of the peace who was tryin' te murder me, was a wee bit slow in hes movements, an' it was just as well too for it give me a chance te dodge hes blow an' grab a hoult of hes baton. The nixt time he wielded it a was fastened te the en' of it, flutterin' like a flag at a royal procession.

He was a very ingenious fellow all the same, so he promptly changed hes tactics an' dashed me te the groun' an' proceeded te jump on me. This was wan of them occasions that calls for quick reactions for he was eighteen stone, so a had te do a most unladylike thing te save me life. A bit him in the bollox an' it rendered him insensible.

Wheniver a got me breath back a thought that a should escape but a seen we were surrounded so a took the only course open te me. A dashed over te the back of an' open Black-Maria an' leapt right inte it. A was just in time too for as soon as a got in they banged the doors an' we headed aff way the siren roarin'. We niver stapped till we reached the Bridewell where they herded us out an' locked us up. It took them a long time te find anythin' te charge us way, so they started te quiz us about where we lived an' who we worked for in order te arrange way their aftercare service that we would have no homes or jobs te come back te when they let us out.

After a while they sent the Legion of Mary in te mingle among us te try te fine out if any of us had souls worth salvagin'. Wan pious legionary spinster way a pioneer pin an' a very red nose took a special interest in my welfare an' wanted te know if a was a minor. A assured hir several times that a wasn't but she didn't believe me. Then a toul hir that she only had te ask anybody who knew me an' she would find out that a was in fact a steeplejack.

That's a most unusual occupation for a young lady

she said earnestly, so a toul hir that a was no ordinary young lady, but a highly recommended, superior, respectable, good-livin, young, Irish catholic business-lady. She then proceeded te prepare me for what she warned was goin' te be a great shock for a nice young girl like me, be tellin' me that when a was brought along te me cell for the night a was te keep me eyes closed an' pass no remarks on things that a seen that were ugly. Just offer it all up te our dear lord, an' it will soon be all over she advised, pushin' a wee holy medal inte me han' te keep me safe.

Wance a got inside the cell a could see what she meant, some prostitutes had vented their spite on the walls way their fury at bein' locked up an' they had some very interestin' observations te make about some of their clients — well-known Dublin dignitaries, includin' high rankin' members of the church an' state.

As soon as a had finished me sex education, a felt a need te go te the lavatory an' a foun' wan sittin' at the foot of me bed. It looked like an ordinary enough lookin' lavatory te me till a was finished an' started lookin' out for the chain. It didn't take me long te surmise that there wasn't any, so a thought it must be wan of these new-fangled lavatories that had handles te turn or buttons te push so a set te searchin' for the knob or whativer, but me search was as long an' as fruitless as it was thorough, an' a finally admitted defeat. Then as if te add insult te injury, me two cell mates had the same urgent need te use the minagery at the foot of me bed as a'd had. They were both better fed mortals than me so the result of their movements was even more offensive than me own, but a offered it up for the sins of the worl' an' went an' lay down on me bed.

When we were first brought te the cell, me two socialist sisters made the democratic decision, that seein' as there were three beds an' only two mattresses, a could have the wan without, that was made outa bare boards way a wee raised bit at the tap for a pillow.

A tossed an' a turned very little indeed for fear that a would do mesel' a terrible injury, but nivertheless a managed in the en' te slip inte an easy sleep. It didn't last long, talk of a rude awakenin', a thought it was the en' of the worl' an' Peter blowin' hes trumpet. Me two cell mates looked startled too, but wan of them managed te point te the bottom of me bed at the thing she called the loo, an' scared as a was, a was curious too, so a jumped up quick an' rushed over te it in order te get a better look at the magic happenin'.

As a stood gazin' in, me mine went back te a day some years earlier when a'd took me wee four year oul sister out for a day, an' set hir up for the very first time on a W.C. When she was finished a lifted hir down an' pulled the chain, an' the wee soul looked in at it in amazement an' then looked up at me an' said, Ann, where is all that pee comin' from? Well, there a was in a similar state of bewilderment — where had all that shit gone — an' how — an' why?

A didn't have long to reflect for a could hear the sound of chains, an' keys bein' rattled, an' big bolts bein' moved. The door of the cell creaked slowly open an' wan of the ugliest creatures of the opposite gender te mesel' that a had iver seen in me life, stuck hes head in the door an' threw three battered tin mugs containin' some liquid of a dubious nature down on the floor. The ugly head then withdrew, an' seconds later reappeared way three crude newspaper parcels which he disposed of in a similar manner. Breakfast was served.

Deo Gratias, a said. A can see we have a wit here, he growled. Naw, a said, not a wit, a classical scholar, ye great ugly lookin' eegit ye. He banged the door so hard that it nearly fell down aff its reinforced hinges an' then he drove the bolt in like he hoped it would niver come out again. A said te mesel', Ann, ye'v done it again, an' set down on the floor te ate.

165

Now a'm equal te most challenges, but a must admit that that was wan of them times when a was beat. A unwrapped me newspaper parcel an' way some delight discovered inside, bread that looked ordinary enough, apart for the odd bit of print on it here an' there, but as a hadn't dined for twenty-four hours that didn't bother me too much, so a bit inte it. A chewed it for a while, an' then for while more, but a didn't seem to be makin' any impression on it.

Now any other bread that a had iver chewed before had put up no resistance, so a started te suspect that though it looked like bread all right it wasn't bread atall. The other two had attempted te wash theirs down way the beverage provided, so a watched them both carefully, an' on observin' subtle changes in their physical appearance (wan of them turned green in the face), a decided not te let on te mesel' that me belly was meetin' me backbone, an' te forgo the pleasures of feastin' for the time bein'.

When our family were all wee wains, we used te grumble an' complain a lot, mostly about things we didn't have, an' other people did. Ivery time we complained, me ma would say te us, god knows ye's are a lot better aff than many other poor creathures, starvin' way hunger an' dyin' way diseases, an' not a roof over their heads, ye's should thank god for what ye's have, an' know ye's could be a lot worse aff, an' mine this, when ye's go out inte the worl' an' have te deal way the hard stranger, ye's might look back, an' realise when it's too late, that ye's had little te complain about,

Well, as soon as a had finished me attempt te ate, the cell door opened again an' me name was called out, an' a turned aroun' an' a knew, that a had at last come face te face way the very hard stranger me ma had warned us about all them years before. He was seven degrees worse lookin' than the waiter who had served breakfast — an' he was wieldin' a set of

166

han'cuffs. He promptly grabbed me right wrist, an' before very long there was this bond of steel joinin' me te him, for better or for worse. A decided te make the best of it an' folly him wheriver he wanted te go — a just hoped that he didn't have te urinate.

He pulled me down a long smelly corridor, an' then down a lot of slimy wet steps that led te the bowels of the earth. He didn't seem inclined towards conversation, so after a while a decided that it was up te me te be sociable so a said te him, a can see you're the strong silent type. When he made no reply te me courteous compliment, a decided te try him way another. A said, a think society should be very grateful te the likes of you for performin' such a worthwhile task, helpin' te clean up the streets an' lock all the villains away. A'm sure we could niver pay ye enough for what ye do, but ye must get a fair amount of job satisfaction te make up for the poor pay. If ye ask me anythin', a think ye deserve a medal.

Now, it's niver easy te carry on a wan-sided conversation, but they say that god likes tryers, so a carried on on that account. A said te him, ye know what's wrong way us criminals, don't ye? We're always ready te consider the worst about iverybody. Would ye believe what a thought about you at first. A thought that you were lackin' in common civility an' courtesy be refusin' te participate in a bit of friendly chatter, but sure it's now just occurred te me that it can't be often that ye come across such a ferocious criminal as me, an' a have ye so scared stiff that the fear has made ye mute.

We were passin' by a naked light bulb, so a looked up into hes face te see how he was takin' it, an' a could see that he was not amused. He was no fun te be way atall so a sadly decided that we must part. While a was slippin' me han' outa the han'cuff a kept on talkin' te distract him be askin' him nice an' politely was he be any chance atall related te Queen Victoria? Ye

167

know, a said, a have seen all kines of rare things in me time but a have niver in me born days seen anythin' te equal that bangle that ye'r wearin', can ye tell me what that strange hoop is hangin' from it for? Then a turned an' run back the way we had come.

He caught up way me after a long chase, an' eventually he dragged me inte court. It was a very solemn occasion. The polis were there, readin' outa their notebooks things about us, that made us sound very much like themsel's. We were all charged way a most horrendous crime — watchin' an' besettin' outside the American Embassy at Pembroke Road, Dublin.

All of us were asked, how de ye plead te the charge? We had te answer, wan at a time, guilty yer honour, guilty yer honour, guilty yer honour. It sounded sorta monotonous like the rosary on a rainy night. A was the eighth along a line of eleven, so when my turn came a said, guilty but insane, yer great lord highship.

A was the only northern felon in the dock an' me accent musta startled him for hes honour stapped what he was doin' (writin' inte a big, oul lookin' book) an' he levered hes glasses far down over hes nose an' peered at me curiously over the tap of them. She pleads guilty yer honour, the barrister said. (He was wan of them nice kind kine of barristers who defended high-powered politicos like me, free of charge.) After we had all finished pleadin', the barrister toul the judge what a wonderful crowd of upright, spotless young characters we all were, but hes highship wasn't convinced — ye could tell — for he sentenced us all te two years' imprisonment — suspended.

Wheniver a landed back at me digs, me lan'lady met me lookin' wile worried, an' a allowed that the after care service must of been in touch way hir. She toul me that she was wile fond of me an' had niver had a nicer person livin' in hir house, but that a would have te lave. She said that if she had hir way a could stay foriver, but hir han's were tied because she was worried about hir children's safety an' hir husband gettin' the sack. A took out the book about Michelangelo that a had got for hir christmas present an' give it te hir early an' went te a bed an' breakfast place for the night.

The man a worked for give me the sack nixt mornin', an' toul me that a was a troublemaker come down from the north te hes nice respectable part of the country, te start upheavals, not bein' satisfied way the trouble a had caused up in Ulster. A toul him te do no en' of nice indelicate things way hes delicatessen.

That day a didn't bother searchin' for a job, a just walked about the city lookin' at the people. A poorly dressed pregnant woman in hir forties, way a pile of scruffy wains, buyin' a badly worn left foot, size four shoe for a penny aff a pile of junk heaped up on a street near the pro-cathedral. Children, naked save for tattered, transparent, waterproof macks, beggin' in the doorway of a city centre pub, fearful of bein' penniless when their drunken parents emerged. Young nuns, starched an' dehumanised, movin' stiffly through the crowds, afraid of bodily contact. Farmers scrubbed an' freshly shaved, down from the country for the day to sell cattle, hopin' to catch the eyes of lovelorn nurses after their work was done. A mother fingerin' prayer beads in hir pocket on hir way home from the pawn shop. A child smacked hard across the face for handlin' toys in a supermarket. 'Please give generously an' god will reward you' boxes shoved under noses, by well-fed, well-dressed, well-past middle-age ladies. Punch-ups about places in a bus queue. Invitations to walk roun' stores with no obligation. Why not visit our movin' crib? — bring all the family — great reductions. A black english student cryin' on the doorstep of a boardin' house because the lan'lady didn't like the colour of hir skin. A mean-mouthed woman dressin' down a teenage girl for wearin' a maxi-length coat. A hungry youth oglin' cream buns in a baker's window. A mother stoppin' traffic on O'Connell Street because hir toddler was missin'. The vacant eyes of a young drug addict who'd got lost forever on a bad trip. And the people with the answers to all the problems of the land, toutin' their propaganda sheets for nine pence a copy outside the historic General Post Office.

After walkin' for several hours, a stapped te take me bearin's an' foun' mesel' standin' over chattering waters on O'Connell Bridge at twelve a-clock on a winter's night, way nothin' te show for me twenty-two years, but a suitcase (half) full of books, an' a self-inflicted education, lookin' inte the Liffey, an' wonderin' what te do nixt.

A could see 'Anna Livia' movin' beneath me, resolutely, determinedly, headin' outa Ireland, an' a knew then that a too must do the same an' go to a place where life resembled life more than it did here, but that like 'Anna Livia' my mind would never quite escape the compellin' god-forsaken shores 'of my fool-driven land'.